SHANNON LOOKED SQUARELY AT THE MARSHAL—

"What are you really after, Manning?"

"Law and order, that's all," answered Manning Cordell. "Justice!"

Shannon eyed him with open contempt. "Where's the justice in shooting down unarmed men?"

"It's all in the point of view," said Cordell. "Look, Shannon, you just tend to your saloon and play your piano. The law is on my side, not yours. Don't meddle. Don't make me come after you."

"You won't have to. You bring in any more dead men across horses and I'll come after you. And that damned marshal's badge won't slow me up a bit."

WILL COOK

KILLER
BEHIND A
BADGE

An Avon Original

AVON BOOK DIVISION

The Hearst Corporation

959 Eighth Avenue—New York 19, N. Y.

As WAS HIS HABIT each evening at seven, Bob Shannon left his hotel, crossed the street and walked a few doors down to Big Bessie's Place, where he had his supper of chili beans and a double rye whisky. This was the beginning of Shannon's day, and it would not end until four in the morning; his office was a piano stool and a battered upright that had once graced a St. Louis bank president's home.

He took his beans and whisky and placed them on the top of the piano, then folded back the keyboard cover and struck a few chords. Bob Shannon was crowding thirty, an age when most men ask themselves searching questions about the value of the things they are doing and the ultimate goal in their lives. Shannon never bothered himself with these trifles. He was a self-contained man, a quiet man who still managed to give the impression that the hell he had raised was all behind him. His manner was always courteous, and people put him down as a fixture, which suited him. Seemingly, he had no outstanding future, and he never talked about his past—but there was a past, and Big Bessie knew it because inside the piano, within easy reach, was a loaded .44 suspended on a hook. At first she had figured this to be only an affectation of Shannon's, but in time she noticed that the .44 was always well-oiled, free of dust and loaded with fresh cartridges.

Bob Shannon worked while other men played and slept while other men worked, and this inverted existence made him into a man with few close friends.

And it was because of this, Shannon supposed, that he had been selected jury foreman; it was a job no one wanted, especially in a case where the prosecution was asking for the death penalty.

He sat at the piano and, with his right hand, softly played a lilting melody that came to his mind; with his left he spooned beans, and now and then he sipped his whisky. The saloon was quiet. High Pockets McGee walked around with a box of fresh sawdust under his arm, sprinkling it on the floor. And Mulloy, who handled the bar trade, washed the beer taps down with soda. It was a quiet, reflective time of the day, when family men went home and lonesome men found solitude unbearable.

Shannon stopped playing long enough to take off his coat. He was very tall and very thin, as though he had once been desperately ill and had barely recovered. His hair was dark on the top and gray at the temples, and he wore a full, sweeping mustache. His clothes were quality cut, and his white shirt had a double row of ruffles bracketing large pearl buttons. For a touch of whimsy, he wore red silk sleeve garters which had once supported the stockings of a shapely Texas fandango dancer. She had neglected to tell Shannon that they were a gift from a lover, and two nights later he had been forced to reach inside the piano for the .44. Afterward, he saw no point in staying in town, so he caught the first stage out, three jumps ahead of the dead man's angry friends.

He sat at the piano as though idly passing time, as though waiting for someone. His wait wasn't long. Heavy steps rattled a few loose boards in the porch; then a man came in, followed by another, much younger but obviously related.

They went to the bar first, and the older man bought whisky while the younger one waited. Then he bought a drink, and the older man paid for both of them. They came over to Shannon, pulled chairs away from a table and sat down. Again, the older man sat first and the younger one followed.

The old man was fifty, blocky in the face and shoulders; there was about him the humorless stamp of hard work, and the first time you looked at him you knew that he had never heard a joke he thought funny enough to laugh at.

"I've been expecting you, Jefford," Shannon said. He nodded to the younger man and struck a final chord, then swiveled around on the stool and faced them.

"We've got to have a little talk," Jefford Lane said softly. "I know you ain't supposed to discuss the trial with anyone, but this thing needs talk."

"What is there to talk about?" Shannon asked. "A man stole your horse and the marshal caught him. Now he's being tried for it."

"I've got four hundred horses," Jefford Lane said. "Hell, one horse isn't worth hanging a man for."

Shannon's shoulders rose and fell. "Suppose he stole ten horses?"

"Well, that'd be different."

"How different?"

Jefford was irritated by this, and his manner showed it. "I didn't expect an argument."

"Well, I don't know what you want," Shannon said. "How do you know what the verdict is going to be? I don't, so don't dig his grave before he's been hung." He turned back to the piano and played softly. "Jefford, I know for a fact that you've personally hung two horse thieves. Why get so stirred up now?"

"Times have changed," Jefford Lane said. He unbuttoned his coat and searched his pockets for a cigar. A heavy gold watch chain sagged across his stomach, and a shell belt and revolver burdened his waist. After he snipped off the end of the cigar, he put it in his mouth and waited, and his son Harry quickly struck a match and held it so the old man could get his light. Lane puffed on his cigar for a

moment, then said, "I'd give a hundred dollars to know
what the verdict is going to be. And another hundred to
know why Manning Cordell is pushing for a hanging."

Shannon turned his glance to the banjo clock ticking
away on the wall. "Manning will be here at exactly seven-
thirty. We always have a drink together before the night
begins. Ask him then."

A frown came to Jefford's heavy face. "I've always
thought it odd that you're so thick with Cordell."

"We're friends," Shannon said, "probably because neither
he nor I have many. You and I are friends, Jefford. I see
no point there. The government appointed Cordell the U.S.
Marshal, and he's doing his job."

"He's hell for hanging," Harry Lane said. He was near
Shannon's age, but he was Jefford Lane's son, which didn't
allow him much of a mind of his own or a way of his own.
He glanced at his father as though seeking silent permis-
sion for having spoken at all, and, when the old man made
no objection, he went on. "I've got nothing against Manning Cordell, but he's only been a marshal for six months
now, and it don't seem right for a man to make his reputation all at one time."

Shannon glanced from one to the other, then finished his
beans and whisky. "You know what the trouble is with
you two? Your conscience is bothering you, and I'm not
talking about a guilty conscience, either. Jefford, you saw
Perkins looking your horse over when he was tied out in
front and told him to get the hell away. And later, in the
stable, Harry saw him again. All right, your testimony was
damaging. What about it? He was caught riding the horse
thirty miles from here, wasn't he?"

Shannon looked past them as the doors swung open and
Manning Cordell came in. He was a man of medium height,
not very heavy, and he wore a dark suit and flat-heeled
boots. Before his appointment as U.S. Marshal he had
been a clerk in the courthouse, and many people in Cedar

Springs were surprised that the government had made a law officer of him. Yet somehow he fit the job, for he was a quiet, dedicated man in his middle thirties, always serious and very thorough in the things he did. Not many people could recall a mistake Cordell had made.

He came over to the group near the piano and pulled another chair around so he could sit down.

"I hope you're not discussing the trial," he said.

"We were talking about you," Jefford Lane said frankly.

Cordell's bushy eyebrows lifted in brief question, then his blunt features settled into an expression of indifference. "Jefford, the prosecutor practically had to drag testimony out of you. Are you getting soft in your old age?"

"I don't like to see a man hang on what I say," Jefford Lane snapped. "Sure, I've thrown a rope or two over a tree myself in past years, but I've got more tolerance now." He shook his finger at Cordell. "And don't tell me you ain't for a hanging, because that's what you brought him back for."

"It's part of my job," Cordell said. He folded his hands and put on an air of patience. "Suppose I asked the court to be lenient? Why, there would be some men who'd take that as an invitation to steal horses." He shook his head slowly. "Sorry, but the law is clearly written; it's a hanging offense, and always will be. If that sounds hard, take it up with the territorial legislature."

"The verdict isn't in yet," Bob Shannon reminded them gently. "You all may be working up a lather for nothing. He could get five years."

"I don't think that will happen," Cordell said, and he got up and went to the bar for his drink. The Lanes watched him for a moment; then they stood up together.

"You can't move that man when he locks his mind on something," Jefford Lane said. "But I still hate it, putting a man's neck in a noose. I'd rather catch him and do the job myself than put it off on some other man to do for me."

He turned and walked out, and Harry Lane hung back long enough to say, "Charlotte's at the hotel, Bob."

"Tell her nine o'clock."

He nodded and went out as Manning Cordell came from the bar with his drink. He sat down. "I didn't scare them away, did I?"

Shannon laughed. "Manning, nothing scares Jefford Lane." He turned to the piano and played softly. "You're going to have a nice report to send to Washington."

"I always send in a good report," Cordell said. "Bob, are you with me or not?"

Shannon laughed. "Getting lonesome?" He paused to light a cigar. "Saw a hanging once. I hope they bring in a verdict of not guilty."

Cordell frowned heavily. "Is that the way you're voting, Bob?"

Shannon laughed. "Now you know better than to ask me that." He tapped his glass on the piano to draw the bartender's attention. "Mulloy, will you bring me another?" Then he glanced at Cordell with some amusement. "You're taking your job too seriously, Manning."

"And you don't take anything seriously enough."

"Why go to all the bother?"

The question annoyed Manning Cordell, for he evaded nothing, good or bad. "Do you want to be a piano player all your life? You know, for a fact, I don't know what else you *can* do."

"I'm a man of many talents," Shannon said. "But I like piano playing the best. I get twenty per cent of the profit here. Can I complain about that?" He played a few trilling notes; he liked to follow the mood of his conversation with music, like a theater pianist punctuating suspense or tenderness. "I've been in Cedar Springs two years now. The first night I hit town I had about three drinks too many and sat down at the piano and played *Dixie*. Big Bessie, being an unreconstructed Rebel, offered me a job at sixty dollars a month, which was nearly twice what I'd earned in other occupations. My talent and my inherent honesty led me into a partnership. Now I call that advancement, Manning." He suppressed his smile; he enjoyed teasing Cordell, because the marshal was incapable of seeing any humor.

"You could have gone into banking," Cordell said.

Shannon had decided that this was the way Cordell's mind worked—along practical, functional lines; Cordell was a man who calculated everything for an effect that was most beneficial to himself.

"You're looking at a man who's happy in his work," Shannon said.

Cordell said, "Bob, I'm not sure whether I envy you or resent you. Sometimes I think a man like you, a man who lets the rest of the world slide by, is a damned menace. And at other times, I think you're a lucky bastard."

The marshal turned his head as the swinging doors opened; a young man came in and stepped up to the bar. He was towheaded and was not quite old enough to shave regularly, and his clothes looked like hand-me-downs. He wore a ragged brush jacket and a bone-handled pistol, and he had the air of a man who has traveled a long way and is about at the end of his rope.

"Whisky," he said, and looked around the room.

Rising, Cordell crossed to the bar. "Sonny, how old are you?"

"Seventeen," the boy said.

"That's a little young for whisky," Cordell said. He exposed the badge pinned to his vest. "I'm the U.S. Marshal. What's your name?"

"Ben Clayton." Then he looked at Mulloy. "Do I get my whisky or not?"

"Give him his drink," Bob Shannon said, leaving the piano. Mulloy hesitated, but only for an instant; Shannon was twenty per cent boss, and Mulloy never argued with the boss. When he set the drink on the bar, young Clayton glanced at Cordell as though to see what he would do. When the marshal turned away, Clayton downed the drink.

Shannon went back to the piano, and Cordell followed him.

"Bob, don't ever interfere with me again."

"Aw, cut it out," Shannon said flatly. "Don't let your job go to your head. When a man drops money on the bar, he can buy what he wants, and, when he's seventeen, he knows what he wants."

There was a silence while Cordell thought it over, making up his mind whether he should argue or not. Then he smiled. "I guess you're right. It's just that I don't like to see a young fellow start wrong." He buttoned his coat. "You want me to order dinner tonight?"

"I'm going to be busy," Shannon said.

Cordell frowned a moment. "Ah, Charlotte Lane. Don't get too thick there, Bob. Jefford wouldn't like a piano player in the family."

He went out, and Shannon turned to the piano again. Mulloy began to polish the bar. Young Ben Clayton lounged around for a while and then went out, his spurs ringing against the porch.

The upright face of Shannon's piano was open, and two mirrors had been mounted at angles to the left and right, giving him an unobstructed view of the saloon behind him. Big Bessie came through the hanging beads from her quarters in the back. She was a woman of undefined age, very heavy and always powdered excessively. Her flesh was soft, and it hung in wattles under her chin. When she walked, her steps were deliberate and solid, as though each one were a chore.

As she came up behind Shannon, she saw his eyes watching her in the mirrors. Bessie waved to Mulloy to bring her some beer. He brought her a half gallon pitcher; she drank directly from it.

"The way you look in those mirrors," Bessie said, "I'd say you either have a curiosity as to what's going on in here, or there's something behind you that you haven't stopped looking for yet."

"You're too nosy, Bessie," Shannon said. "Manning just left."

"I saw him," she said. "That's why I didn't come out. Bob, don't get too thick with Manning." She planted her heavy arms on the piano top and glanced down at the .44 hanging there. "If he knew about that, he'd wonder why you keep it hanging there. And he'd start digging, and, if there was anything in your past worth running from, he'd find it out. Then he'd turn on you."

"If there's anything in my past," Shannon said, "it's personal. The law doesn't want me for even spitting on the sidewalk."

"Yeah, well, keep it that way. And Bob, you do what Manning wants. Be better that way."

He frowned. "What do you mean, Bessie?"

"This horse thief affair—you go along with Manning. Take an old woman's advice; I know the Manning Cordells."

At a quarter to nine, Elfrieda Danning came in, and Bessie took her pitcher of beer and went back to her quarters. Elfrieda was a tall, blond woman in her early twenties, and she wore a flowing dress, tight at the waist and breast. When she whipped off her shawl and folded it, she revealed shoulders both white and smoothly muscled.

"Another day, another dollar," she said to Bob Shannon. There was a little rye whisky left in his glass, and she drank it, then leaned on the piano top and looked at him. "If you gave me a raise I could get out of here a lot quicker."

"What's your hurry?"

"We're all in a hurry to do something or other," Elfrieda said. She had a face a little too squarish to be classical, yet her features were good. Her eyes were dark and the lashes long, and her lips were firm and full without appearing petulant. She wore only a trace of powder, and there was a faint scent of perfume about her. "Bob, will you please play *Chicken Reel* when I'm not here? If I hear that tune once more, I'm going to yell."

"The customer is always right," he said softly. "I'm a piano player and you're a faro dealer. Be happy, Elfrieda. The world is a funny place." Her purse, a cloth affair, was on top of the piano, and he reached for it, opened it and took out her bankbook. "Eight hundred and fifty-two dollars and sixty-one cents." He put the book back. "How much money do you need?"

"Two thousand," she said. "Enough to keep me in style for one year. That's how long it will take me to catch the right man."

"Like an undertaker measuring someone for a coffin," Shannon said. Then he laughed. "You could marry me and sing in the church choir every Sunday."

"Not because I'd be welcome," she said, "but because you're the only one in town who can play the organ." She shook her head. "You're too much like my father, Bob. He was a hard-working man; then one day he thought, What the hell's the use, and stopped. He drifted into this town and died, and do you know what he left me?"

"Yeah, eighty-six dollars, and you've never forgiven him for it."

"There's no talking to you," she said, and walked into the back room to see Big Bessie. He watched her until the beaded curtains shut her from view. She was an attractive woman, but without much heart; or perhaps the heart was there, but she had learned to hide it as though ashamed or afraid. He could never figure out which.

Precisely at nine o'clock, Shannon put on his coat and left the saloon, cutting diagonally across the street to the hotel. He went through the lobby and into the dining room, stopping just inside the archway for a look around.

Then he saw Charlotte Lane sitting in the corner, waiting for him. She smiled, a quick, bright flash, and he threaded his way past the tables. He sat down and gave the waiter an order for both of them. Then, when the man had passed from earshot, Shannon said, "I was hoping to see you, Charlie."

She was twenty-five, and many women securely married were already labeling her a fussy old maid, but Shannon thought of her more as being particular. She was not very tall, but she was shapely and soft-spoken, and within her was a deep capacity for laughter. He knew that most of the single men in town were awed by her fathers' land and wealth and that they stayed away from her because they knew what it was like to tangle with Jefford Lane, but Bob Shannon never thought about these things. He saw her about once a month, when she came to town, and it was a bright interlude in his life, something he kept warmed over until he saw her again.

Her hair was like ink, framing a smooth, round face, fine eyes and lips as soft as a man could dream of kissing; he often wondered what it would be like to kiss her, but somehow the opportunity had never presented itself.

"Are you staying overnight?" When she nodded, he added, "Let's not talk about a horse thief, Charlie. I only see you once a month, and I don't want to waste it."

"It could be more often than that," she said. "You know where I live, Bob."

He smiled. "Sure, but Jefford wouldn't like to see a piano player sitting in his parlor on a Sunday afternoon."

"You're more than a piano player," Charlotte said. "And isn't this something we're going to have to settle one of these days?" She looked at him steadily, and he thought how strange it was that this should come up when he least expected it. They had never spoken of their feelings toward each other; he was not at all certain of what she thought of him, and he didn't dare to hope for more than her friendship.

"How do we settle it?" he asked. "Almost two years ago I saw you sitting in this hotel lobby and asked you to have dinner with me. It was a bold thing to do, but we've had nineteen meals and they've been memorable."

"And all the thinking and hoping in between," she said.

"Yes, there's been that, too."

"That's why we have to do something, Bob. We've got to come out with it or not see each other again." She touched his hand lightly. "Why did you come to Cedar Springs? What were you before you came here? A good man, I know, but what were you?"

The waiter came with their food, and Shannon waited until he moved out of earshot. "Right now, I wish I'd been someone important, Charlie; when I talk about it, it doesn't seem like much at all. I've worked cattle, drove stage and been a law officer. Company C, Texas Frontier Battalion. Two years there, Charlie. I thought for a while that I'd make a career of it, but I changed my mind. There was some trouble near Lampassas. The sheriff telegraphed for the Rangers, and I was sent. When I got there, he'd been killed and the bunch that did it were holed up. One against five is poor odds, Charlie, and they were desperate men who'd killed before, so I took them by surprise at night. It was like killing hogs, and, when I got back to the company, I resigned." He shrugged. "You know the rest because I came here not more than a month later." He put his napkin beside his plate. "Are you hungry? Neither am I. Let's go some place—for a walk, anything." He saw no refusal in her eyes, so he got up and pulled back her chair for her.

As they started to leave, the waiter came from the kitchen, saw the untouched food and said, "Something wrong, Mr. Shannon?"

"No, everything's fine," Shannon said, and taking Charlotte's arm, walked out and down the street with her. The traffic was moderate, for Cedar Springs was a crossroads town and a lot of people came from somewhere, bound for somewhere, and only stopped to rest and spend a little money.

The street farther down was dark, and they walked along, then cut over a block to the courthouse lawn, with its big trees and the path running past the cannon standing guard around the flagpole.

They sat down on the cement and stone base of the cannon. Just behind them was the courthouse, and, around to one side, the small jail containing the prisoner now on trial. Shannon started to light a cigar, then thought better of it and put it back in his pocket.

Charlotte Lane laughed softly. "Now, if you were thinking that I might not like the taste of a cigar when you kissed me, you'd be wrong, Bob."

That she had so accurately plumbed his reasoning came as a shock. It struck him funny, and he laughed. "I thought I was less obvious than that." He touched her on the arm, then pulled her against him and put his arms around her. "You're right, Charlie, we have to do something."

"Uh-uh—*you* have to do it."

She put her hands on his face, and he kissed her—gently, to show her he had restraint—but under the compelling softness of her mouth his restraint vanished, leaving him with a raw desire. He pulled away from her before he made a mistake.

"I won't break," she said, smiling.

"I always handle new things gently," he said.

"Can I expect you for supper Sunday evening?"

"Try and keep me away," Shannon said. "And I'll tell Jefford, understand?"

"All right, but I'll soften him up, if that's at all possible—"

She stopped talking suddenly, and Shannon turned his head to see why. A man was approaching from the street side, leading two horses. He passed within thirty yards of them, heading around the side of the courthouse toward the jail. There was a lamp on in the marshal's office, and when the man darted in front of it Shannon recognized him as Ben Clayton.

For a moment Shannon could not understand what Clayton was doing; then it dawned on him that he was about to engineer a jail break.

"Stay here!" he said, then changed his mind. "No, better go back to the hotel. And find Manning Cordell."

As Shannon started to leave, Charlotte grabbed his arm. "Bob, don't try to do anything alone."

"Get out of here; there's no time to argue."

She obeyed him, and he turned toward the jail, wishing that he had his pistol. But it was a poor time to think of that; he'd have to do what he could without one.

Clayton was crouched by the door, and a match sputtered as Shannon approached. A fuse ignited and fizzed brightly, and then Clayton wheeled and ran, bumping squarely into Shannon. The two men went down in a welter of arms and legs, and Clayton whipped out his gun and tried to hit Shannon on the head with it. Shannon caught Clayton's wrist, and they rolled, struggling for possession of the gun.

And then the dynamite exploded, ripping the main door right out of the stonework. Clayton couldn't linger now; the noise, like a fire gong, would draw a crowd. He laced a punch at Shannon's jaw and ran toward the jail, leaving his bone-handled pistol in Shannon's hand.

Shannon saw Clayton and the prisoner run out, and he flipped the gun over in his hand, catching it by the butt. He carried them in his sights all the way to the horses; then they thundered out of the yard, taking the first road out of town.

A crowd was coming on the run, led by Manning Cordell, who hauled Shannon roughly to his feet as though he were responsible for the whole thing.

"Why the hell didn't you shoot?" Cordell asked. He snatched the pistol from Shannon's hand and looked at it. "Haven't I seen this before?"

"It belongs to Ben Clayton. He lost it while we fought." Shannon shook his head sadly. "Sorry, Manning, but I just couldn't shoot two men in the back. I had them cold all the way, but I couldn't pull the trigger."

"Well, get your horse. Mine, too—he's in the stable. They can't be far ahead." He gave Shannon a shove. "Come on, you owe me that much after fumbling everything here."

"I suppose you've got a point," Shannon said, and pushed through the crowd to go back to Big Bessie's.

• 2

SHANNON TOOK HIS TIME about telling Big Bessie where he was going, then went to the hotel to change his clothes, roll his blankets and get the holster and belt for his .44 Colt. When he got back to the porch, he found Jefford Lane there.

"When you get back I want to talk to you," Lane said.

"All right," Shannon said. He found a boy loitering nearby, gave him a dime and sent him scurrying to the stable for the horses.

Manning Cordell was coming down the steet with angry strides.

"Where's the horses?"

"A kid's going after them," Shannon said.

Cordell looked at the holstered pistol. "Where did you get that?"

"It's mine," Shannon said.

"I didn't know you had one," Cordell said.

"You don't know everything, Manning," Shannon told him. Lane was still hanging around, looking for a crack into which he could wedge talk. This irritated Shannon; he turned to Lane and snapped, "If you've got something to say, then say it!"

A crease deepened in Lane's forehead. "I don't like that tone."

"That *is* too bad," Shannon said, and stepped off the porch to meet the boy, who was coming with the horses. Mulloy came out of the saloon with a sack of provisions. Shannon took them, and then the two men turned out of town.

They took the west road that led across the broad valley floor to low-crouched hills. This was ragged, uneven country. On all sides foothills rose into more prominent heights, and at this time of year the highest peaks wore a mantle of snow, which glowed whitely in the night light.

Cordell seemed to know where he was going, and Shannon wondered what the marshal was thinking, how he was reasoning this out. Then Shannon decided that Cordell was figuring that Clayton and the escaped man would go into the hills instead of riding south and entering the plains country. He knew that Cordell was a proud, sensitive man and that this jail break had cut him deeply; it was a bad thing for a man to put in his report, especially if he failed to recapture the prisoner and the young man who had released him.

Three hours of steady riding brought them to a fringe of stunted timber, and Manning Cordell dismounted, saying, "They'll stop once they get into the hills. Build a fire. We'll have some coffee—if Mulloy put anything in that sack besides whisky." Shannon gathered some dry wood while Cordell talked. "They're both strangers to the country, and Perkins lit out this way after he'd stolen Lane's horse, so I figure he'll do it again just to put distance between himself and a rope." He slapped his hands together and began to crowd the fire as soon as Shannon lit it. "God damn that punk kid anyway! I'm going to put him away for ten years for this. You see if I don't."

"Why get steamed up about it?" Shannon said. Then he laughed. "If they get away, I guess we'll never know what the verdict would have been."

"Hanging," Cordell said. "In all conscience, it couldn't be anything else. And don't tell me Perkins couldn't see the rope dangling. This break was arranged, all right." He filled the coffeepot from his canteen, dumped in some grounds and pushed it up to the edge of the fire. Then he stretched out on the ground and looked at Shannon. "I've never seen you wearing a gun before. Can you use it?"

"Good enough."

"Was that your business before you took up piano playing?"

"I took that up at the age of five," Shannon said. "Two hours of practice every day. Any other business I have is my own, Manning."

"All right, let it go. Tell me, how did the jury vote go? It doesn't matter now if you talk about it."

"Guilty," Shannon said, and Manning Cordell smiled. "Except for me," he said and watched Cordell's pleasure fade.

"What the hell were you holding out for?"

"Because I could see him going to jail, but not being hung. Perkins is only twenty-three, Manning."

"You were going to hang the jury," Cordell said tightly. "What the hell's the matter with you, Bob? I thought I knew you better than that." He blew out a ragged breath and pulled the coffeepot from the fire. "Jesus, how can a man enforce the law when people won't stand behind him? And they've got to respect the law, look to it for justice. I'm from Kansas. My father was shot down in the streets of Lawrence by a drunken teamster who got fined eighty dollars and run out of town. Four years later my oldest brother was shot to death during a bank holdup; the robber escaped and was never caught. That's the kind of public backing I won't tolerate. By God, I'll either get justice through the courts or I'll find some other way."

"There isn't any other way," Shannon said.

"For a man who plays tunes in a saloon, you've got some firm opinions."

"Could be," Shannon said. "Clayton lost his gun, and I don't think Perkins had time to grab one; they may be unarmed."

Cordell laughed without amusement. "Bob, desperate men are always armed." He finished his coffee. "By the time I retire, it won't be necessary for a man to protect himself. You think that's a foolish brag?"

"No, but meanness is hard to pare out of a man." Shannon kicked the fire to smoldering rubble, then toed dirt over it. "Let's get going, huh? You may be sure you're going to catch them, but I'm not."

"They'll go into the badlands," Cordell said. "A man always feels safe with rocks around him." He waved his hand to include the land beyond. "That's all Jefford Lane country. Kind of ironic, to be trapped on his land, since stealing his roan got them into this mess in the first place."

"I'm not looking for irony, just to catch them and take them back." Shannon stepped into the saddle.

They used up the rest of the night making their way through country that grew continually more difficult. They passed above timber line a few hours before dawn, Cordell in the lead, slowly picking his way among the rocks, clinging to a trail that was little more than a goat path along a sheer rock face.

It was, Shannon had to admit, the kind of country that a man would choose to hide in, and he had to admire Cordell for his shrewd judgment; the man was a good hunter—

patient, steadfast in his purpose and completely dedicated
to his duty. Most men would have turned back or taken
an easier, more roundabout route, but Cordell was not like
that. He kept crowding in, guided by logic and instinct.
Shannon knew that this was what people meant when they
called certain law officers manhunters.

"There's an easier way through this country," Shannon
said.

"I know it. And more than likely they've taken it. But
this way I'll end up ahead of them. They probably followed the valley floor through Lane's land, but by dawn
we should be where they are."

"Where's that?"

"On the old north road."

Cordell's horse faltered on the rough trail and nearly lost
his footing, and Cordell cursed and pulled him up.

"Watch yourself, Bob. A fall here could be bad."

"You're the one who slipped," Shannon said.

They were moving along in those black, pre-dawn hours
and Shannon closed up a little with Cordell because he
could not see more than three or four yards ahead. How
Cordell could keep up his pace was a mystery to Shannon.
The marshal seemed to have cat's eyes, picking out the
thinly marked trail as though he had a second sense.

The trail dipped down and Shannon sighed with relief,
figuring the worst of it was over, but he figured wrong;
going down was at times more difficult than climbing. The
horses slid on stiffened legs, and once Shannon checked
what started to be a bad fall.

The sky was just beginning to turn gray in the east, and
a chill wind began to blow, moaning through the rocks
and raising swirls of dust. Cordell reached behind his saddle
and tried to get at his coat without bothering to stop and
dismount for it. He got it partially loose, then jerked it
free, and it flapped, frightening Shannon's horse.

The animal jumped, half rearing, then lost its footing

and fell into a roll, going completely over Shannon before he could kick free. He cried out and felt a bone snap; then the horse fell clear of him and stood trembling at the edge of the trail.

"God damn!" Bob Shannon said, and clutched his left leg.

Cordell immediately dismounted and dropped his reins. He half lifted Shannon and said, "Get you bad?"

"Bad enough. I think my damned leg is busted."

"If I get you on your horse, do you think you can make it to Jefford Lane's place? It's only eight or nine miles from here."

"Hell, do I have any choice?" Shannon gritted his teeth until a spasm of pain passed. "I know you too well to expect you to stop now and pack me back."

"You know I have a job," Cordell said. He looked at the sky. "Be broad daylight in another forty minutes. If you're careful, you'll hail the ranch house in five hours."

"That'll be dandy," Shannon said.

They wrapped the leg in Shannon's coat, and used a rifle for a splint and both their pants belts to hold it in place. Cordell shouldered Shannon into the saddle and saw him off on the back trail, all within thirty minutes of the fall.

Gathering the reins, Cordell stepped into the saddle and rode on, the growing light allowing him to increase his pace. He was sorry that Shannon had taken the fall, yet he was glad he hadn't been held up by it. Taking Shannon along had been a notion of impulse that Cordell had regretted, because Shannon didn't see things the right way; he entertained a tolerance for other men that Cordell didn't have at all. Yet he liked Shannon about as well as he had ever liked anyone, because there was a mystery about him that he couldn't quite solve. Shannon was more than a piano player, and exactly what he was bothered Cordell.

He worked out of the rough country all that mid-morning, and, when he came to the slash marking the old road, he hid his horse in the rocks and hunkered down, intending to get a little sleep. The way he figured it, young Clayton and his friend would come along that road very soon; it was the shortest distance between Cedar Springs and Twin Falls, where they could catch a train clean out of the territory.

Only horsemen used this road now, the wagon and stage traffic having taken a dogleg west to touch another town before dropping south to Cedar Springs. Yes, it was rough country for rough men in a hurry—just rocks and rattlesnakes and lizards and stunted brush.

In his mind, Cordell went over the time and distance problem facing young Clayton and the escaped prisoner. Forty-six miles, by the old road, from the courthouse to the summit, a spot near Cordell's hiding place. They ought to be showing within an hour, if they were going to show at all, and Cordell was betting everything that they would.

He wanted to build a fire and fix something to eat, but he pushed the thought from his mind and thought about Bob Shannon; he would be halfway to Jefford Lane's ranch by now, then tucked into a soft bed and made comfortable while a doctor was fetched from town. That was the way Cordell figured on going back; he'd stop at Lane's and spend the night there before riding back to Cedar Springs.

There'd be just time, too, if Clayton and Perkins didn't show up late. He looked at his watch and found the hands high—nearly noon. Finally he heard a sound, a shod hoof on rock. Easing his pistol from his holster, he peeked from behind the boulders and saw them coming along slowly, carefully, no longer watching their back trail, because they believed they were in the clear.

When they were twenty feet from him Manning Cordell stood up, and both men halted, staring at him, surprised to see him, angry because he had outguessed them.

"You really didn't think I'd let you make it, did you?"

Cordell asked. He motioned with the pistol. "All right, off the horses and hands high."

"Don't get nervous," Perkins said. "Neither of us has a gun."

"That's what you get for leaving in a hurry," Cordell said. He looked at Ben Clayton and then at Perkins, seeing a slight resemblance between them. "You two kin?"

"Brothers," Clayton said. He sighed and scuffed dirt with his boot. "I suppose I'm going to jail now, too."

"Both of you have caused me embarrassment," Cordell said. "I try my best to maintain law and order, but it seems that everyone's against me. The jury couldn't seem to agree to hang you, and then you had to go and break jail."

Perkins' face brightened. "You mean I was going free?"

"You stole a horse," Cordell said. "You ought to have been hung two weeks ago." Then he looked at Ben Clayton. "And you wanted to make me look bad to my superiors in Washington so they'd think I couldn't handle the job. Now I've got to do what a jury didn't do."

For a moment they did not understand his meaning. Perkins understood it first and started to turn, to run, but Cordell shot him through the chest and dropped him there, then turned the gun on Ben Clayton. The boy was flung back by the bullet, and he raised his head from the ground and looked at Cordell pleadingly before he died.

Punching the shells from his gun, Cordell reloaded and holstered it, then took young Clayton's gun from his hip pocket—the same gun he had taken from Shannon in town —and dropped it in the dust beside Clayton's still hand.

"Now," Cordell said softly, "I won't expect any more trouble from either of you."

He turned then and fetched their horses so he could load them on, take them back, bury them and write out a proper report.

3

THE PAIN, the real pain, didn't start until about an hour after the fall; then Shannon found it almost unendurable. There were times when he knew he was never going to make it to Lane's ranch at all, but he kept telling himself to hang on, that it wasn't any worse than that time on the Brazos when he'd ridden eighty miles with a bullet in his side.

Two of Lane's riders found him on the broad valley floor, about a mile and a half from the main buildings. Shannon was barely conscious when they lowered him from the horse, and he could not really remember one of the men going for a wagon and half a load of hay. The ride into the ranch proper was fog that his mind could not clearly penetrate, but he remembered vaguely being undressed and put to bed and the doctor setting his leg. He was given ether and blessed sleep, and when he woke up he was violently ill. The leg was in a plaster cast over the knee, and he could move it without feeling a thing.

It was evening; he could tell that by the long shadows in the room and the crowding darkness. Harry Lane came in and put a match to the lamps; then he saw that Shannon was awake.

"Decided to come back, huh?"

"I'll pass up any foot race that comes along," Shannon said. "What time is it?"

"A quarter after six. Do you know what day it is?"

"Friday?"

Harry Lane laughed. "Sunday. Well, you told Charlotte you'd be here; you're a man of your word, Bob."

Jefford Lane came in; the old man stood by the bed and looked at Shannon for a moment.

"Awake, I see." He smelled of cigar smoke and horses, and there were gray ash spots on his vest. Pulling a chair around, Jefford Lane sat down. "The marshal came through yesterday."

"It was the day before, Dad," Harry said.

The old man shot him an impatient glance, then said, "Well, whenever it was. Around sundown. He got both of 'em."

"I figured he would," Shannon said. "You don't ever want to figure that Manning can be shaken off." The odor of cigars about Jefford Lane woke hungers in him for a smoke, and the old man, sensing it, offered Shannon a cigar and a light. After a few puffs Shannon sighed and said, "Man, that tastes mighty good. I wish I'd been awake when Manning was here. Too bad about young Clayton. He made a desperate try, and now he'll have to serve time for it."

"A damned long time," Lane said. "He's dead."

Shannon looked at him as though he had heard wrong. "Dead? How could that happen?"

"They're both dead," Harry said. "They put up a fight and Cordell fought back."

"Well, I've got a ranch to run," Jefford Lane said, rising. "If you want anything, just ring the hand bell on the table. One of the servants will answer you."

He went out and closed the door. Harry remained seated, one leg crossed over the other. "Pa wasn't happy when he found out you and Charlie were spoonin' in the courthouse yard."

"He sounded unhappy the night I left town," Shannon said. "Harry, did you see Clayton and Perkins?"

"Sure, why?"

"Were they shot from the front or back?"

Harry Lane frowned. "Now that's a damned impolite question. They were shot from the front. Why? What do you think Manning Cordell is?"

"I'm not sure now," Shannon said. Then he smiled. "How's everything with you, Harry?"

"The same. I get my wages every month, just like any other hand. And I'll go on getting them until Pa dies."

"My offer still stands," Shannon said. "Two thousand in cash. You can go somewhere else and get a start."

Harry thought about it, as he had always thought about it, but his answer was the same. "As long as I stay here I can't lose, Bob. And for that I can take the bossin' and the cussin's and the foot kissin'." He smiled without humor. "I'm no gambler. Pa knows it, and that's why it's no trouble to keep me under thumb." He pushed back his chair and turned to the door. "If he's left the house, I'll send Charlotte in."

"Let's not be sneaky about it," Shannon said.

"Is there any other way to do it?"

After Harry Lane went out, Shannon turned his thoughts to Cordell and a cold-blooded killing, and he wondered what he was going to do about it. Facing Cordell with what he knew would only yield satisfaction, because Cordell was the law and people would believe him, even applaud him for capturing two criminals. Anything Shannon said against Cordell would be made out as a lie. He didn't like the way this was shaping up; he'd given up being someone else's champion, yet he knew himself and knew he couldn't stand by and see things go to hell without doing something. He just wasn't a sideline man, able to keep his nose out of business that needed fixing. Well, he supposed that had been all right as a Texas Ranger, but for piano players it was no good at all.

And he hated like hell to think of giving up the piano to go back to law enforcing.

The door opened and Charlotte came in; she smiled and sat on the edge of his bed, then bent over and kissed him lightly. "You need a shave," she said, and rubbed a hand against his beard stubble.

"I could do without this broken leg, too," he said. "Have I been much trouble?"

"You're never any trouble," she said, laughing. "All I wanted was for you to come to dinner, and here you are—a house guest."

"Don't take this wrong, but I'd just as soon have come for dinner and let the other go," Shannon said. He hunched himself up until he was sitting, and she fluffed the pillows at his back. "Did your father say anything to you about the other night?"

She shook her head. "I think he's saving it for you."

"Mmmm, I figured that. Do you want me to spit in his eye, Charlie?"

"Would you? No one's stood up to him in twenty years."

He looked at her steadily. "He doesn't scare me, but I want you to understand what it would mean. I'm a partner in a saloon, and the best I could offer you is a five-room house in the so-so part of town. You'd have to do your own washing and cook the meals."

"I'm not helpless, Bob."

"That tells me what I have to know."

He looked past her as a servant opened the door. Charlotte said, "What is it, Emile?"

"A buggy from town."

"The doctor?"

"No, it's Miss Danning."

Charlotte Lane frowned and got up. "I'll see what she wants," she said, and left the room. Through the closed door Shannon could hear them talking; then it stopped, and Elfrieda came in.

"Well, look at you," she said, and took off her hat.

"You drove out to see me," Shannon said. "Isn't that sweet?"

"Don't think I'm getting soft in the head," she said. "I just want to know when you're coming back to mind the store. Big Bessie doesn't tend to business, Mulloy's already cutting the drinks and putting the profit in his pocket and those two dealers you hired last month are shaving the edges of their cards."

He smiled. "Are you still running a straight game?"

This angered her, and she spoke tightly. "I ought to poke you in the mouth for saying that. You know I go by the rules, Bob. Like it or not, that's the way it is."

"All right," he said. "I wasn't trying to insult you. Why do you defend yourself all the time?"

"Because I won't be close to anyone," she said. "You always get hurt that way, and it's no damned good."

"Someday you've got to learn to forgive."

"Let's not start on that," she said. "When can you leave your bed of pain?"

He shrugged. "Doc Windham put a heavy cast on my leg, with a metal loop on the bottom so I can walk. Maybe in a few days."

"You're losing fifty dollars a day over the bar, and, when the word gets around that your games are crooked, you'll have real trouble. Now, if you think getting your head stroked by soft hands is worth that, you just stay there."

"As a wife you'd be hell," Shannon said. "Nag, nag, nag." He waved his hand and threw back the covers. "My clothes are in the closet." He let her help him up. He felt dizzy for a moment, but it soon passed. He had to cling to the bedpost while she helped him dress, and he was tucking the tail of his shirt into his pants when the door opened and Charlotte came in.

"What are you doing out of bed?"

"I've got business in town," Shannon said, "and it can't wait."

"Who dressed you?" She glanced at Elfrieda Danning. "Is this your idea?"

"If you allow him to lay around, he'll get lazy," Elfrieda said, and put her arm around him. "Now let's see you walk."

He took a step and found it not bad at all; he just had to swing the stiff leg along.

"Bob, you fool, this isn't good for you!" Charlotte said. She took Elfrieda's arm. "You just want him away from me, that's all!"

"I wouldn't have him as a gift," Elfrieda said flatly. "But if he doesn't tend to business, I won't have a job—and, honey, I'm not going to lose my pay because he has a broken leg or you have a case of sweet young love."

"That's enough!" Shannon said. "Go on out and wait in the buggy."

"You're a heartless person," Charlotte said. "I feel sorry for you, Miss Danning."

"Now you've ruined my day," Elfrieda said. "Completely." She went out, got in the buggy and sat there.

"She's right about the business," Shannon said, regretfully. "Those two card players I hired a while ago are cheating already, and Mulloy is stabbing his hand in the till because he doesn't know any better." He put his arms around her and kissed her. "I'm going to talk to Jefford just as soon as I can." Then he kissed her again and hobbled out to the buggy. He tossed his pistol belt on the seat and got in, and Elfrieda turned around and headed back to town.

They rode in silence for about a mile; then she said, "Are you going to marry her, Bob?"

"Now let's not get nosy."

"It would be a mistake," she said softly. "You could never give her what she wants."

"How do you know what she wants?"

"That's easy enough to see. She wants you to take her away from her father, just to have someone do it. Afterward she'll grow unhappy with you—or any man—because she really doesn't want to leave that big house and servants and money. She just wants to show her father that she *can* leave."

"What a miserable way to look at things," Shannon said.

"It's an honest way," she said. "And I like that better than the pretty way. And so do you, Bob—so why fuss about it? Manning knows how to solve his problems, doesn't he? They're burying the Clayton boys this afternoon."

"I guess you could call it a solution. Some people might think it a good thing if a mad dog bit every bad person, but who gets rid of the dog?"

She frowned at him. "What are you talking about? Manning?" She thought about it for a moment. "I get your point. It must have been some fight, with one gun between them."

"And which one of them had the gun?"

"Ben, the young one. It's a bone-handled forty-one, and Mulloy gave Manning forty dollars for it to hang over the bar."

"Ben didn't have that gun," Shannon said. "He dropped it in the courtyard, and I picked it up and gave it to Manning in the street. If Cordell says Ben had it, he's either lying or gave it back after Ben was dead."

Elfrieda believed him because he had never lied to her. Still, she was shocked, even frightened, by what this meant. "Now I really know what you meant about the mad dog," she said, and looked at him. "Are you going to face Manning with this?"

"I have to," he said. "Manning's no good, and all of a sudden I know it and no one else does. That singles me out, Elfrieda. It makes me responsible, in a way." He smiled thinly. "Most of my life has been spent taking care of other people's troubles. I had the notion that I wanted to quit that business, but I guess I was fooling myself."

"I always knew you were more than a piano player," Elfrieda said. "And it's too bad. I could even learn to like *Chicken Reel*."

4

Wʜᴇɴ ᴛʜᴇʏ sᴛᴏᴘᴘᴇᴅ in front of the saloon, the two men who had been standing there talking came to the edge of the walk. One of them said, "What does it take to slow you down, Bob?"

"I'm slowed down," Shannon said. "Give me a hand out of this rig, Sam." He grunted when he touched the ground, then hobbled across the porch and into the saloon. Mulloy was in the back room, and when he heard the peg leg thumping he came out; his mouth dropped open a little, but he couldn't find anything to say.

"Where's Haskell and Davis?" Shannon asked.

Mulloy nodded toward the hotel. "Sleeping. They had a good night."

"How about you?" Shannon asked. "Did you have a good night?" He glanced at Sam, who was standing just inside the door with his friend. "Go over to the hotel and wake both of them up. Tell them I'm here looking for two cheating cardsharps."

Both men ducked out, and Mulloy asked, "What's got into you, boss?"

"You and those two sharp card dealers," Shannon said. "I'm gone a couple of days and you try to rob me blind. What the hell, Mulloy, how much did you think you could take?"

"Who says I took—"

"I said it," Elfrieda snapped. "You want to deny it?"

Mulloy said nothing; he just looked at the pistol belt Shannon was carrying and grew a little worried when Shannon buckled it on, settling it against his hip.

"You know," Shannon said, "I'm not much, and I have a

lot less, but I'm honest. I don't lie, cheat or steal. I can't be bought into or bought out, and I can't stand around and have it done under my nose. You've been dipping your big hands into the till, and those two paper peddlers have been dealing from the bottom." He shook his head sadly. "Mulloy, I thought you knew better than that."

"What are you going to do?"

"I'm going to have it out with Davis and Haskell."

"For a few lousy dollars?"

"Yeah, because they weren't your dollars—or theirs."

They waited, Shannon leaning against the bar, and pretty soon Buck came back. "They think it's funny, but they'll be over."

"Then you stand out of the way," Shannon told him.

"I'll give my share back," Mulloy said. "Hell, Bob, this is the first time I ever done anything like this." He spread his hands in an appeal. "I've got a wife and three kids!"

"Congratulations," Shannon said.

He could see out the open door, and he observed Davis and Haskell as they crossed the street. They entered boldly and saw him standing at the bar. Haskell smiled.

"What is it the piano player wants? You really ought to apologize, if that local character quoted you correctly."

"If he called you cheating cardsharps, he was correct," Shannon said. He looked at Davis. "Have you got your little trick derringer rig up your sleeve?"

"I sleep with it," Davis said, smiling, too. He pointed to the gun Shannon wore. "That's a little unaccustomed, isn't it?"

"I put it on for special occasions," Shannon said. "How much did you get?"

Haskell shrugged. "No need to keep it a secret. I got nearly three hundred, Davis a little over two. And we like it. We've decided that it's the way the games are going to be run from now on." He tapped the hard metal spring rig in his right sleeve. "This says so."

"Does it? I've never seen one of those things work. Use it."

He couldn't beat it for speed; no man could, for they were lightning fast, but the range was twenty-five feet, a little long for a two-shot stinger. Davis fired, and the bullet pimpled the bar an inch from Shannon's sleeve. Then Shannon wiped the .44 out of the holster, rolled his thumb across the hammer as it came level and knocked Davis clean off his feet. Even as he swung the gun toward Haskell, the man's arms shot straight over his head; clearly he wanted out of this—a long way out.

Davis rolled on the floor, moaning with a fractured shoulder, and Shannon said, "Get the money and put it on the bar. I'll wait."

"It's in the hotel," Haskell said nervously.

"I said I'd wait, but don't keep me waiting more than five minutes." He stood there while Haskell wheeled and ran across the street.

Big Bessie waddled from the back room to see what all the shooting was about, and Mulloy stared at Davis, who was in great pain.

"Can I go for the doc, Bob?" Mulloy asked.

Shannon nodded, and Mulloy ran out. Big Bessie puffed up to the bar and said to Elfrieda, "Honey, will you draw me a pitcher of beer? That's a good girl, dearie." She stared at Davis, who was bleeding in the sawdust. "Good thing High Pockets didn't put down new."

Manning Cordell came running down the walk and burst into the saloon. He looked at Davis, then at Shannon. "What was this all about?" He used a hard, rough tone that angered Shannon.

"We were proving that the hand was quicker than the eye," Shannon said. "And he lost."

"I'll have to arrest you," Manning said flatly.

"You'll play hell," Shannon told him. "Davis shot first

and I've got witnesses, which is a hell of a lot more than you have to support your story."

The only change in Cordell's expression was a tightening of the flesh around his eyes. He said, "Suddenly I have a dislike for piano players." Then he turned and went out.

As soon as Doc Windham came, Shannon hobbled over to the piano and sat down. He hung his .44 on the peg and sat there, not at all pleased with himself, or the way he had handled the two gamblers. Haskell came back with the money and insisted that it was all there, every penny. He wanted to count it, but Shannon waved him away.

"Just get out of town and forget you ever heard of Cedar Springs."

This was sterling advice that Haskell intended to take; he went to his room to pack.

Elfrieda brought a bowl of hot water and a razor from Bessie's room and put it on the piano. Shannon said, "What's that for?"

"So you won't look like the last rose of summer." She put a towel around his neck and began to work up lather in the mug.

"I can shave myself," he said. "You'll cut my throat."

"I used to shave my father," she said. "It made him feel important to have someone shave him. There were plenty of times when he didn't have a quarter for beans, but he managed to have a barber shave him." She lathered his face, soaked a towel in hot water, and wrapped his head in it.

With Mulloy's help they got Davis out of the saloon, but before the doctor left he came over to the piano. "Was that a lucky shot, or did you aim there?"

"I wouldn't kill any man for two hundred dollars," Shannon said.

Windham smiled. "Now I feel better about the whole thing."

He left, and Elfrieda took away the cloth and began to

blade Shannon's face clean. When the razor pulled he took it away from her, stropped it on his belt and finished the job.

"You stood up hard to Manning Cordell," she said. "He hates you now."

"He never really liked me much anyway," Shannon said. "There isn't much like in a man like Manning." He looked into his mirrors while shaving and saw Cordell pause in the doorway again. To Elfrieda he said, "Find something else to do."

She hesitated, then walked over to the bar, where Big Bessie was sipping her pitcher of beer. Cordell came to the piano, toed a chair around and sat down so that he could face Shannon.

"It's hard to think of you as an enemy, Bob."

"I'll leave it up to you," Shannon said. He toweled his face dry, then took a cigar from his pocket and lit it. "Manning, I gave you young Clayton's gun. You ought to have known I'd never let a thing like this stand."

"I don't remember you giving me his gun," Cordell said. "You can't prove it."

"No, it's my word against yours, and they'd believe you before they believed me. What are you after, Manning?"

"Law and order," Cordell said. "We've got to straighten this out between us. I don't want to have to go after you."

"Where's the justice in shooting two unarmed men?"

"I'll give any criminal what he deserves, and that's justice." He leaned forward and spoke gently. "Bob, tend to your saloon and play your piano and let me run my business. You know what I stand for."

"Manning, there's going to be no more dead men brought in across horses. Do you understand that?"

"No man runs my office," Cordell said. "Don't interfere. You're not a lawman."

"Manning, I was a Ranger when you were filing papers in the courthouse basement," Shannon said angrily. "I was hunting men by the time I was twenty-one, and I've locked up more dangerous gunfighters than you've ever heard of." He stuck his finger under Cordell's nose. "And I'm man enough to come after you, if I have to, and that damned government-appointed marshal's badge won't slow me down a damned bit. You lie when you say that young Clayton had a gun, and now I wonder about those three men you brought in early this spring. Now watch yourself, Manning. And don't be a fool and shrug this off as a threat made to you by a piano player."

Cordell shied his chair back to the table and stood up. "All this fuss and breast-heaving over a couple of saddle bums."

"Two dead men, Manning."

"It's all in the point of view," Cordell said, and went out.

Shannon could not understand the man's coldness, his complete lack of sympathy; Cordell possessed a passionate reasoning that pushed aside regret or consideration for anyone else. There were times, Shannon knew, when it took that kind of a man to bring law to a territory—a man who could kill coldly, like some laborer in a slaughter house, untouched by his environment or the reasons for his work.

He knew that Manning Cordell would ignore the warning, and it was only a matter of time, now, before they had to face each other. And the outcome of that encounter would be uncertain, for, good or bad, Cordell was United States Marshal, and no man put one to the gun without having a wanted poster printed up on him and hung from Maine to California.

It was a weapon in Cordell's favor, an immunity that wouldn't be done away with lightly.

5

Manning Cordell made the courthouse at Cedar Springs his headquarters because the county had no sheriff. He found the office comfortable, as well as being centrally located, yet he spent quite a bit of time away from Cedar Springs; his authority extended over a wide sweep of land, and he took his duties very seriously.

And in Big Bessie's Place, Shannon played the piano, listened to the run of talk and found, by and large, that everyone was pretty well pleased with the way Cordell handled things. In his lifetime he had listened to a lot of talk like this, especially when a country was rough and the people had never lived under the benefit of law and order; anything looked good to them then—even a combination judge, jury and executioner like Manning Cordell.

Big Bessie's business was picking up. Some of the ranchers to the south, who were driving their fall herds to the railhead, found Cedar Springs a nice stopover to kick up a little fuss and run the boredom out of the system. A small outfit was in town, trying to drink the place dry and spend all their money before they got it, but at three o'clock Bessie closed the place, as she always did, and locked the front door. She went to bed, leaving the clean-up to the bartender and High Pockets McGee. Shannon went to the bar, got a final stein of beer and sat down at one of the tables. Elfrieda Danning was taking her shoes off so she could rub her feet. When Shannon put the beer stein down, she took a sip of it, then sagged back in the chair.

"Every night I swear this is going to be the last."

"But in the morning you think of the money," Shannon said, smiling. "It's hell to have ambitions, isn't it?"

"What do you know of ambitions?"

"Oh, I have them," he said. "You may not believe it, but in this breast beats the noblest of hearts. Some day I must tell you the story of my life, dedicated to lofty purpose and purity."

"Sort of a fantasy, huh?"

"You are a born cynic," he said and drank some of his beer. "Manning is quite a hero, isn't he? If you believe public opinion." He found a cigar in his pocket and put a match to it, then sat there, puffing contentedly. "I knew a man like Manning Cordell once. He just got bigger and bigger, and the things he said became more and more important until there wasn't any truth, just what he said."

"So what happened?"

"A twelve-year-old boy shot him," Shannon said. "The boy curried the big man's horse, and then he refused to pay up. In anger, the boy threatened him, and the gun went off."

"And they hung the boy," Elfrieda said.

Shannon shook his head. "No, they didn't know what to do, so they had a statue made of the big man and set it on the courthouse lawn."

She frowned. "If your story has a point to it, I've missed it."

"My point is that Manning Cordell could go on and on and not be caught," Shannon said. "A United States Marshal is as high as you can get as a law enforcement officer, Frieda. And just a plain run-of-the-mill citizen isn't going to get very far locking horns with him. Legally, Cordell can overrule a lot of local officials—like the city marshal, if we had one—and the mayor and local judge. But he'd have trouble bucking a county sheriff."

"We don't have one."

"Yes, and it's a damned shame," Shannon said. "The whole thing is that Cordell is exercising authority in county matters, which is all right since we don't have a county sheriff. I'd like to take some of his business off his hands."

Elfrieda Danning looked at him; then she said, "How do you mean?"

"Well, Cordell is going to be hard to talk into a hole, but if we had a sheriff, a good man, maybe a few people would see the difference between real justice and Cordell's kind."

"Election's a year off, and since old man Ennis died no one seems interested in running."

"A man could be appointed," Shannon said.

"You?"

"Why not? I'm experienced." He leaned forward, his manner intense. "If I had the backing, I could get that appointment. And I know a man who will bargain."

"Jefford Lane," she said. "He's the wealthiest man around here, and people will jump when he whistles. Bob, are you sure you want to do this?"

"It's my town now," he said. "Frieda, it isn't always what a man wants to do; it's what he has to do because he might be the the the only man who *could* do it. It's not pleasant to know a man like Cordell, knowing, too, that you're tough enough to put him down. You know that and you look at yourself closely and ask yourself what keeps you from being like him, and sometimes the answers are hard to find." He sighed and finished his beer, leaving a little in the bottom, which Elfrieda drank.

"I figured it up the other night; it'll take me a year to get out of here," Elfrieda said. "I'll be twenty-four." She met his eyes seriously. "You're not the only one looking at yourself, Bob."

"Yes, but you're prettier." He took the stein, hobbled to the bar and put it in the sink. Mulloy was counting up the cash; he gave it to Shannon, who went in the back to Big Bessie's quarters. She was sitting by her dresser unrolling the stockings from her fat legs, and she looked at him in the mirror when he stepped inside.

Bessie said, "That girl would look better in a kitchen than behind a faro box."

"She'll get there; give her time."

"In many ways, you're a fathead." She waved at the money box. "Have you counted it yet?"

"No, but it feels heavy." He put it on her dresser. "Bessie, if I can swing it, I'd like to go back to my old business for a while."

She frowned, then said, "A good piano player is harder to get than a sober husband." Then she shrugged. "But I've learned not to hold a man to his bargains, so go if you want to."

"I want to leave the door open for me to come back, Bessie." He sat down and rubbed his hands together. "I want to go after the county sheriff's job."

She nodded. "You've just got to get Cordell, is that it? Oh, he's never fooled me with that bring-'em-back-across-the-saddle business. He's a conscience killer, Bob. They're hard to stop because they think they're an instrument of divine providence." She slipped into a pair of old, soft shoes and padded around the room looking for a cigar. This was another of her bad habits, but she never let the public know about it. Shannon and Elfrieda Danning knew, but if anyone else came into the room and smelled the aroma of a cigar, Big Bessie always said that a caller had just left by the back door. And since her life was full of callers, no one questioned her.

"Cordell's like a good horse that bolts and starts to run," she said. "Then he finds out that he can resist the pull of the reins and goes a little crazy with his own power. The only thing that'll stop him is a brick wall."

"I know how to lay bricks."

She smiled. "All right, get it done then. But don't keep me without a piano player for too long. Anyone can tell you that I'm faithless as hell where men are concerned."

"All right, Bessie."

He went out and across the street to his hotel, leaving

Mulloy to lock up. In his room he undressed, got into bed and lay there awhile, thinking that tomorrow he'd go out and see Jefford Lane; the quicker this was done, the better.

After an early breakfast and very little sleep, Shannon walked to the stable and tried to decide whether he should take a buggy out to Lane's place, and enjoy the trip more, or strive for an appearance and ride, which would be uncomfortable as hell. He decided to ride, for he was going to dicker with Lane about a county appointment, and he didn't want Lane to think that he was too soft or incapacitated for the job.

He arrived before noon, and Jefford Lane came out as Shannon dismounted. Lane said, "You get around pretty good."

Shannon was saddle-sore, but he didn't let Lane know it. He took a chair on the porch; then Charlotte came out and clapped her hands in pleasure.

"Bob, how nice! You'll stay for supper, won't you?"

"I can't say yet. Perhaps." He glanced at Jefford Lane, saw the old man's displeasure and was glad that he'd given her a flexible answer. When a man came for a favor, he did his best not to get anyone angry. "I thought I'd come out and talk business with Jefford," Shannon said. "If it worked into a supper, I wouldn't really fight it, but business first."

He had hurt her feelings; he could tell by her expression. "Well, I won't bother you then," she said, and went into the house.

"Spirited," Jefford Lane said. "Sometimes I wonder if any man can handle her." He put tobacco in his pipe and lit it. "What's on your mind, Shannon?"

"A new occupation," Shannon said. "The county needs a sheriff, and I've had considerable experience as a law enforcement officer."

"We've got Cordell."

"You don't like Cordell. You'd like me better."

Jefford Lane didn't like to concede any point. He said, "Oh, I get along with Manning all right."

"You hate his guts, so admit it."

"Well, let's say there's no love lost." He squinted at Shannon. "The way you handled those two tinhorns, I figured you must have had some kind of experience, either on the side of the law or against it. What do you want to be sheriff for?"

"Because you need a good one."

"Well, I had a notion of putting my boy Harry up for office at election time."

Shannon knew Lane and the devastating opinion he had of others, even his own son. So he said, "Harry can't cut it, and you know it. But let's say he can. Do you want it to look that obvious, just putting him in office? It would get people to talking, Jefford, and you won't like it. But if you appointed me until election time, then, if Harry ran against me and won, no one would be able to open his mouth and claim that Jefford Lane ran things around Cedar Springs."

"That's smart thinking," Lane admitted. "Shannon, you're a damned horse trader."

"Yes, but I'm offering a bargain with good teeth," Shannon said. "Jefford, you can't control Cordell the way you could a county sheriff. Why, you had to come to me, the jury foreman, just to talk. If Cordell had been sheriff instead of marshal, you could have gone to him, told him you'd liked to have seen Perkins fined or jailed for a spell, and that's all there'd have been to it."

"By God, that's the truth," Lane said. He regarded Shannon thoughtfully. "I like your terms, but I've got a few of my own. I've worked like hell to get where I am, and if I act like I was a little better than the next man, it ain't because I think I am. It's just that a man in my position has to sort of lord it over others or they'll get to thinking he's an easy mark."

Shannon kept a straight face and said, "My, that sure is so, isn't it?"

"I always knew you saw it," Lane said. "But my point is that I've got to be careful of the company I keep. My boy Harry has to watch himself; that's why I keep a tight rein on him. And Charlotte—I expect her to marry right at the top, some professional man like a doctor or a lawyer, or someone with a political future. Are you following me?"

"Quite easily," Shannon said. His impulse was to show a little anger, but he forced it back and sat quietly. "What's your proposition, Jefford?"

"That you never get serious about my daughter, Shannon. Or let her get serious about you. Now I've given it a lot of thought, and I guess there's no real harm in you two seeing each other, but I want it kept in mind that she's got to marry better than what's in Cedar Springs. I trust you, Shannon; you're a man of your word. Give me that word and you can take office inside of a week."

"A trade ought to be thought over," Shannon said. "I could have my answer after supper."

Jefford Lane chuckled and slapped Shannon on the leg. "Go in and tell her you're staying," he said.

Shannon had to pause just inside the door to collect himself; a few deep breaths restored his humor, and he went down the hall and into the kitchen. Charlotte was advising the cook and one of the servants, and, when she looked around to see who had come in, a trace of annoyance was still in her eyes.

"Are you leaving or staying?" she asked.

"Staying, if the offer still stands."

"I ought to withdraw it to teach you a lesson," she said.

"And I deserve it," he said.

She smiled then, came to him and took his arm. "You're apologizing. Let's go for a walk. The kitchen is hot."

They went out the back door and across the dusty yard to an orchard of fruit trees, and there they sat down on a bench. "Bob, did you talk to him about us?"

"He agreed that we could keep company," Shannon said, taking the truth out of context.

"Why, that's wonderful! Did he growl?"

"No, he accepted it philosophically. He doesn't think a piano player is exactly what he had in mind for you, so I've agreed to step up a little in social status. I'm going to fill in as county sheriff until next election."

This didn't exactly please her, but, since she was getting her way, she didn't question the matter too much. Harry Lane came out the back door and paused on the porch; then he saw them and walked across the yard. He dressed in the rough denims of a working man, and he liked to think of himself as the hardest-working man on the place, but Shannon knew that the foreman, who liked his job and meant to keep it, gave him the easy jobs and saw that he had a lot of time off because he was still Jefford Lane's son.

Harry rolled a cigarette and raked a match across his belt buckle. "Dad says you're going to be the new sheriff." He shrugged. "Well, I didn't want the job anyway." He sat on the ground, his legs crossed. "Manning Cordell isn't going to like this. He likes to handle everything by himself."

"No man can handle everything," Shannon said. "There's enough county business to keep a man busy. Besides, Manning will have more time to handle Federal matters. In another three weeks, Cedar Springs will be full of cattlemen pushing toward the railhead. There's no need for Manning to bother himself just to keep the local peace."

"There's one thing you've got to say for Manning though. He don't take orders from Pa."

"It might be better if he did," Shannon said. "Jefford Lane has the biggest pay roll around here. If he took his business to some other town, half the stores would close up. It figures that he'll have a lot to say about how things are handled. And there's no crime in it. He's not a monster, Harry." He laughed softly. "Why don't you get away for a while? Try your luck someplace else. In a year you'll think differently."

"Are you still dangling that stake in front of my nose?" Harry shook his head. "I don't want to start on borrowed money." He got up and brushed off the seat of his pants. "I've got work to do."

He walked rapidly toward the barn, and Charlotte, watching him, said, "Poor Harry—I don't think he'll ever really be a man. If he'd only swear or talk back, or—or anything, he'd be all right." Then she looked at Shannon and smiled. "I know my father; he wants to own everything, and everyone. But he doesn't own me. He never will. If I want to do something, I'll do it. And that includes marrying the man I want to marry." She got up and took his hands. "Come on—you've got time to take me riding before supper. And I know a place where the trees are shady and the rocks are high, and you can kiss me without being seen."

• 6

DAYLIGHT WAS GONE when Bob Shannon left Jefford Lane's place. The old man shook hands with him on the porch as though he had just made the biggest deal of his life, and he was still standing there when Shannon rode out of the yard.

He took it easy going back because he didn't want to get his leg to throbbing so it would keep him awake all night. In all, he figured he had had a very successful day; he considered any day a good one when he got what he went after. The bargain he had made with Jefford Lane he meant to keep to the letter, and, if Lane ignored the independent nature of his daughter, then that wasn't Shannon's fault. It was a failing among big, important men, that they were so wrapped up in themselves that they were ignorant of the characters of those closest to them.

The night was dark, so much so that he could barely see the road, but the horse knew the way and Shannon was content to let him pick his own pace. Then he reined up because he thought he saw the bulky shadow-shape of a horse and rider ahead.

"Who's there?" Shannon asked. He didn't want to run afoul of some cowboy coming back from town with a bellyful of Mulloy's whisky and a mind crowded with meanness.

The horseman shifted, and again Shannon asked, "Who's there? Put a match on yourself. This is Bob Shannon."

The last thing he expected was a gunshot, so he was unbelievably startled when he felt the bullet strike the horse in the neck. The animal reared, spilling Shannon, but he managed to roll away before the horse fell.

Shannon was not hurt, but he was stunned. The horse kicked a few minutes, then lay still. In the following silence the rider who had fired the shot turned and headed back for town. Shannon was disappointed; he had wanted the man to come closer, to strike a match for a look, so Shannon could have a look himself. But the gunman was too smart for that. If he had scored, there was no need for a look, and, if he had missed, he still remained unidentified—and he would have another chance.

Finally Shannon got to his feet and, thinking of the long walk back to town, wondered if he could make it. After walking a hundred yards, then pausing to rest, he decided he could whittle away at the distance and maybe get there by daylight.

He knew this would be the last time he'd ever go without his gun; he kept thinking how satisfying it would have been to have swapped lead with the gunman. One thing about walking and sitting—it gave him plenty of time to think the thing out. There were some enemies lurking around from his past, men who'd ride a thousand miles to shoot him, but he seriously doubted that one of them had suddenly shown up. An old enemy, being a stranger, would have waited for him in town. Besides, anyone turning up at this particular moment would be too much of a coincidence.

He didn't have any local enemies, although he was working on it. And the only man who could have a reason for feeling better with him dead would be Manning Cordell. But Cordell was seventy miles away, in another town on business.

Shannon had to admit that it was a very long walk, a hundred yards at a time with a rest in between, and, with his leg throbbing, the rests kept getting longer and longer. But he was a stubborn man who pecked away at a thing, a sliver at a time, and the sky was just turning gray when he saw Cedar Springs in the distance, still a mile away. He thought of a painting he had seen in a Socorro bar—a nude on a sleeping lounge, and, peering through the curtain, a man with a look of anticipation on his face and more than conversation on his mind. Shannon had looked at that picture a hundred times, and the man never got any closer, which was probably why the artist had titled it *So Near, Yet So Far*.

Cedar Springs was like that painting; he couldn't seem to get much closer to it.

As he sat there, massaging his thigh, he noticed a buggy far down the road, just a moving speck beneath a swirl of rising dust. As it drew nearer he recognized Elfrieda Danning. Then she saw him sitting there and increased her speed, finally stopping in a cloud of rank dust.

"Where the hell have you been?" she asked angrily. Then she got down off the buggy. "Where's your horse?"

Shannon indicated the direction with his thumb. "Dead. Somebody took a pot shot at me around nine-thirty." He grinned at her. "You're a welcome sight, Frieda, but believe me when I say that that buggy is *more* welcome."

She helped him in the rig, then turned around and started back. "I didn't start worrying until after midnight," she said. "It was always possible that Jefford Lane would invite you to dinner, but I thought it darned unlikely that he'd let you stay the night." She shot him a worried glance. "Who took the shot at you, Bob?"

His shoulders rose and fell. "I couldn't see, and he didn't say a word. But he was waiting for me right smack-dab in the middle of the road. I called out, told him who I was, then—*bam!* My horse stopped the bullet."

"How did you make out with Lane?"

"I got the appointment," Shannon said. "Lane likes to make deals. I never had much doubt about getting it, as long as Lane figured I'd be *his* sheriff."

She frowned. "You're not anybody's man, Bob. Doesn't Lane know that? I still wish you hadn't bargained with him; he's a poor man to owe a favor to. Besides, there are others in Cedar Springs who could have given you the backing."

"Sure, if I'd taken the time to get them together. And I don't have the time, Frieda. By the time Manning gets back I'll have that badge. Then we're going to talk about jurisdiction; he's going to stay clear of county affairs."

She let him off at the hotel, and he hobbled up the stairs to his room. He washed his face and hands and threw his

coat over the back of a chair; then he sat on the bed.
Elfrieda came in with a tray and put it on the chair near
him.

"Breakfast," she said.

"What are you, a professional mother?" He regarded her
a moment. "It doesn't fit you, Elfrieda."

"No? Why not? Because I plan to be somebody? Bob, my
ambitions don't get in anyone's way. Not even my own."
She got up and stepped to the door. "Now eat and get some
sleep. I'll see you over at Big Bessie's."

After the door closed, he stared at it a moment, then ate
his eggs and potatoes and wondered just how well he knew
her or if he even knew her at all. He lay back on the bed,
too tired to sit up and too full of aches to sleep. The day
had turned off sunny and hot, and a fitful breeze blew the
window shade, making it rustle annoyingly. He heard a
man's step in the hall, then he raised himself on his elbows
as the knob turned.

Manning Cordell stepped in and closed the door.

"You're looking a little green around the gills, Bob." He
scooted a chair around with his toe and sat down.

"When did you get back?" Shannon asked.

"Last night around dark," Cordell said. "Enjoy your
walk?"

Tightness gripped Shannon's chest; then he said, "You're
a lousy shot, Manning."

"No, I'm a good shot," Cordell said. "But it was
dark as hell, and I couldn't see your horse's head in the
way." He looked at Shannon and smiled. "What are you
going to do about it? You going to tell it around that I
took a shot at you?" He laughed softly. "They'd laugh at
you and say you were drunk."

"Manning, you've got it all figured out, haven't you? How
did you know where I was?"

"When I put my horse in the livery stable, I saw that
yours was gone. When I mentioned it to the liveryman, he

said that when a man is courting he don't have good sense. So I knew you were out to Lane's place." He leaned back in his chair, and his eyes drew into veiled slits. "Bob, I don't want to kill you, but you're going to get in my way stopping me from doing what has to be done. Now why don't you pack your suitcase and get out? There are other towns; you'd be happier there."

"Then who'd stop you, Manning?"

"No one's going to stop me," he said. "Bob, I can clean up this country to where it's a decent place for anyone to live in. What am I, some wild animal? Hell, I never shot a man yet who didn't deserve it." His manner grew intense, as it always did when he tried to explain himself, as though he were continually reaffirming his own beliefs. "There's only one thing that the toughs fear—a man who will hunt them down and kill them where he finds them. Let me tell you what happened while I've been away. I was up near Ridge Rock a week ago when the stage came in. Someone had held it up, robbed the passengers of seventy-one dollars and made off clean as a whistle. The marshal there is an incompetent; he shrugged the whole affair off as just one of those things that happen when you have a bad year and someone is desperate for a little money to tide him over. As for the passengers, he didn't seem to feel any responsibility toward them and their loss. Naturally I took the matter out of his hands and went on the assumption that he'd unwittingly told the truth. I looked for a man who'd had a hard year and needed cash, and in two days I found him, living on a small dirt farm. He was surprised to see me, so surprised that he gave me the money back. Now, if I hadn't caught him, Bob, he'd have thought how easy it had been to steal, and the next time he'd have taken more, or stole more often. They're all bad seeds."

"Where is this bad seed now?" Shannon asked. He watched Cordell's eyes, then shook his head. "Never mind, Manning. I know what happened."

"He had a rifle," Cordell said. "What could I do?"

"Where was it? Leaning inside the door?"

"In the tool shed," Cordell said. "Bob, all you have to do is to tell me you'll go; I'll take your word. Make it easy for both of us."

"I can't," Shannon said. "Call me stupid, Manning, but I can't be bought or scared off. I knew a man once who just had to have everything his way. Down in Texas, when I was a rookie Ranger on my first assignment. He ran the town so well that they paid him money for the privilege of living under his thumb. If somebody tried to leave, they got shot. He offered me five thousand in cash to ride out and forget it; all it would have cost me would have been my star and reputation. Yeah, I turned it down."

"And ended up killing him," Manning Cordell said.

Shannon nodded. "Yes, I had to kill him. But that doesn't make us alike." He swung his feet to the floor and faced Cordell. "You want to know why I can't go now? I'm the new county sheriff."

For a moment, Cordell just sat there. Then he laughed, leaning back in his chair to roar. Shannon listened for a moment; then a haze of anger took hold of him, and he hit Cordell, knocking him over backward, spinning him onto the floor and against the wall.

The blow was solid and Cordell was dazed, but he reached for his gun just the same. Shannon swung his leg, the one with the cast on it. From the way Cordell yelled, Shannon thought he must have broken his arm. The gun flew across the room, and Cordell tried to scramble to his feet.

Shannon was at a disadvantage because he couldn't move rapidly, and Cordell hit him twice in the face before he could swing away. Then he swung his leg again and caught Cordell on the shins, hurting the man again; he started to hop around, clutching his leg. Shannon dropped him to the floor with one punch and went after him, mauling him toward the door.

The commotion had brought the curious to the stair landing, and some of them crowded into the hall as Shannon flung the door open. Cordell was still trying to fight back, but Shannon pulped the man's nose with his fist, dragged him to the head of the stairs and flung him all the way down to the bottom.

He followed Cordell down, hobbling, clinging to the rail, and Cordell was standing when Shannon got there. They both swung, bloodying each other's faces. Cordell tried to hit Shannon with a flower pot, but missed and managed only to scatter dirt and plant on the rug.

The cast was a formidable weapon, and Shannon was learning how to use it. He battered Cordell's shins bloody, then caught the man on the rear with a long looping leg swing and propelled him nearly fifteen feet. He went out through the front door, arms flailing, lost his balance and cascaded off the porch into the dusty street. When Shannon followed him, pushing his way through the crowd, his temper had cooled enough for him to look upon the fight with some objectivity, and he saw that he was making a shambles of Manning Cordell.

Cordell's coat was in tatters, and his shirt was ripped nearly off. His face was streaming blood, one eye was completely closed and his breath whistled through the ruptured cartilage of his nose. He was trying to stand, and Shannon collared him from behind and, using his cast to boot him along, kept him moving toward the jail and sheriff's office, followed by a large crowd.

Once inside the building, Shannon slammed Cordell into a corner; the man was too sick and dazed to protest. Then Shannon took everything that belonged to Cordell and threw it in the street. Clothes, books, personal effects—everything littered the area outside the door. From the wall he took a double-barreled shotgun and loaded it; then he pointed it at Manning Cordell.

Shannon said, "Now go find yourself some other hole

to roost in. Go on—get the hell out of here, Manning!"

Cordell roused himself and stumbled toward the door. There he paused and pointed his finger like a gun; he opened his mouth to speak, but no sound came out. He wheeled then and, using his fists to smash his way through the ring of onlookers, went on down the street.

One of the men standing there, said, "What was that all about?" He looked at Shannon and waited; then, getting no answer, he shrugged. "Hell, I was only curious," he said, and turned away. The crowd started to break up, and in a few minutes Shannon was alone.

He hadn't intended to plant his flag so quickly or solidly, but Cordell's laughter, the fact that he took another man so lightly, had acted as a trigger to set Shannon off. He knew what he had to do now, and he didn't like it. He'd have to play Cordell's game and make the man fear him, just as Cordell worked to make others afraid.

It was the only weapon the man would understand.

• 7

Doc WINDHAM FOUND Shannon washing and inspecting the cuts on his face; he stopped in the open doorway and knocked, then stepped in and said, "The front yard looks like a bunkhouse after a twister hit it. Is all that Manning's stuff?"

"Yes," Shannon said. He turned away from the mirror and washstand. One of his eyes was badly puffed, and he had a gash on his chin that wouldn't stop bleeding and another across the arch of his forehead. "Is this a professional call, Doc?"

"Well, after taking care of one, and noticing the condition he was in, I thought it would be good for business to

look in on the other." He smiled and opened his satchel.
"Come on over here and sit down. Where the light's better.
That's fine." He examined the cuts. "Going to have to make
a couple of stitches, Bob." He got out all the things he
needed and went to work, talking all the while. "That
must have been made by Manning's ring. A wicked weapon,
a ring, if it's shaped right."

"How is Manning?" Shannon asked.

"Are you being solicitous? Or do you just want to gloat
over the damage?" He shrugged. "He's hurt. Flat on his
back when I left him, and I don't think he's about to get up
for a day or two. Boy, you lit into him good. Were you
trying to kill him?"

"Maybe I was," Shannon said. "He tried to kill me."

Windham laughed. "He didn't do so well. Outside of a
few cuts and bruises, I'd say he hardly damaged you."

"I'm not talking about the fight," Shannon said flatly.
"Manning tried to shoot me last night on the road in from
Lane's place."

"You're joking," Windham said. Then, "No, I guess
you're not. Is that the truth?" He shook his head in
puzzlement. "But why would Manning want to do a thing
like that? Give me one good reason."

"You wouldn't believe it."

"Give it to me anyway."

"Because he's a killer," Shannon said.

Windham's expression didn't change, but he put away
his needle and sutures and, by not saying a word, said everything that needed to be said.

"See, I told you you wouldn't believe it," Shannon said.

Windham snapped his bag shut. "Bob, we all know Manning better than that. He's a good law officer. Hard, yes,
but still a good man." Then he looked around the office.
"What are you doing in here, anyway?"

"It's mine," Shannon said. "I'm the new sheriff, until
you elect another one."

"Who says so?"

"Jefford Lane will say so."

Windham grunted. "Well, Jefford usually gets what he
wants. Who am I to say it isn't good?" He put on his hat
and went out, stepping gingerly through the rubble outside
the door.

Shannon sat down in the heavy oak swivel chair and
looked about the room. He'd jumped the gun a little, and
he wasn't sure whether Lane would like it or not, but he
really didn't give a damn. Jefford Lane might be a hard-
pratted old war horse, but he kept his word. Come hell or
high tide, Shannon would get his badge.

He knew authority was a formidable weapon; most men
automatically respected it. He had found this so as a
Texas Ranger, when he had been sent to a town or a part
of the country to settle trouble. That badge on his coat
was enough to quiet all but the most foolhardy. It gave a
man swinging room when he had to cut someone down and
a sort of absolution afterward when he looked on what
he'd done.

Manning Cordell would take the badge as a challenge,
and Shannon hoped that the marshal was filled with enough
hate to make him careless; he wanted Cordell to charge
him in a free-for-all showdown.

Late in the day he sent a boy to the hotel to bring his
things back in a wheelbarrow, and, after putting them in
the side room, he sent the boy to Big Bessie's place with a
note. When the boy came back, he had Shannon's .44 in a
paper sack. A quarter sent the boy on his way, and Shannon
took the gun apart, oiled and cleaned it and reassembled it.

At a glance, the .44 was not much different from others
sold over the counter from Albany to Sacramento. But if a
man knew guns and knew the men who handled them, and
knew the skilled German mechanics who worked in little
shops and created something special, he would admire
Shannon's .44 right off.

The ejector rod and housing had been shortened three-quarters of an inch. The barrel had been cut to an equal length, bringing the balance back into the butt so that it sat well in the hand—not with the heaviness forward to kill the weave, but with the muzzle light so that, when it was palmed fast, the bore came quickly to line, ready to be squeezed off.

All the lockwork was glass-honed, and the hammer had been changed so that the spur, with a wide, very lightly knurled surface, fell a little lower; it was nearly as broad as Shannon's thumb. The heavy leaf mainspring was gone; it had been replaced by a cleverly built plunger and tightly wound coil spring, which made the hammer feather-light to cock, yet very fast and strong on the fall. In all, capped by yellowed ivory handles, it was a masterpiece of deadliness, in proper hands.

And Shannon had the hands.

That evening he had his supper brought to the office. He knew the town was talking about the fight and about his appointment as sheriff. A lot of them wouldn't like it because, when the cowboys came in, they didn't want any foolish laws to spoil the fun or lessen the ringing of the cash registers. The last man who had held office had been pretty reasonable, but that was no assurance that the next man would be. Which, Shannon figured, was the one big reason a man hadn't been elected or appointed.

Jefford Lane came into town rather late, stopped at the saloon for a drink, then came on to the courthouse. He was frowning, not unpleasantly, but with annoyance. And he came right to the point.

"Got an early start on Cordell, didn't you?"

"I didn't think you'd mind," Shannon said blandly. "You've often felt like hitting him yourself."

"Well, that's the God's truth," Lane said. "I'm going to talk to the mayor and town council tonight. We can get this settled with very little fuss. I can't think of anyone

who would buck me in this thing." He scratched a match
for his cigar. "One of my riders spotted several big outfits
driving this way. They ought to hit town late tomorrow
night or early the next morning. Now, I want a liberal
policy, Shannon."

"Naturally."

"Well, all right. I just didn't want any misunderstand-
ings."

"There won't be," Shannon assured him.

Jefford Lane consulted his watch. "I'll have the judge
come back with me to swear you in. Say around ten-thirty?"

"I'll be here," Shannon said.

Lane went out, his step heavy. Shannon wheeled his
chair around and cocked his feet on the filing cabinet.

From the doorway, Elfrieda Danning said, "Yes, Mr.
Lane, no, Mr. Lane. Aren't your lips sore from kissing his
cuffs?" Shannon turned the chair around and smiled. Elfrieda said, "I heard him talking and waited. Shannon, he's
not a soft old man, so watch him."

"I intend to." He motioned to a chair. "Did you sleep
through the fight?"

"Yes, and what the devil got into you? From what I
hear, you really beat him up." She shook her head as
though she were trying to deal tenderly with a precocious
idiot. "I thought you had better sense." She reached over to
the desk, lifted the coffeepot and felt the bottom. "Cold.
Well, I'd better get back to Big Bessie's. There are some
drovers in town with fifty dollars and an itch to buck the
cards." She got up, went to the door and, pausing, turned
around. She saw that he was wearing his gun and smiled
in agreement. "That's a good idea; sleep with it in your
hand from now on. Cordell's going to be coming after you."

"I want him to," Shannon said. "It's the easiest way."

"Sometimes it can turn out to be the hardest. Ask me,
who always loved the easy way."

After she left, Shannon poked around the desk drawers

and cabinets and found nearly eight months of unopened mail, all addressed to a sheriff now dead; no one seemed to care enough to send out notices, let alone answer these. He tried to sort through the stuff, to restore some order, and he was busy at it when Jefford Lane and Judge Robbins returned. Robbins was only a county official, and not very effectual, but he had authority enough to appoint a sheriff or issue a restraining order.

"I'd like to offer my congratulations," Robbins said, extending his hand. "I'm sure you'll be a courageous officer, devoted to duty and always cognizant of your civic responsibil—"

"I'm a little pressed for time," Jefford Lane said, cutting Robbins off. "Can't we get on with the swearing in?"

"To be sure," Robbins said. "Would you stand over there, Mr. Shannon? Thank you. You'll be the witness, Jefford. Everything legal, you know." He smiled, then began to intone the oath.

Shannon listened and repeated and swore to everything, then was given the badge and the power to arrest and appoint deputies. Robbins thought it was too bad no one had a bottle so they could drink to the official occasion, but Lane solved it by taking him over to the saloon and standing treat.

After they left, Shannon remained alone for a few moments, then decided the best thing to do would be to go to the main street and show the people what Jefford Lane had bought for them. He locked the door but left the lamps burning, since he didn't figure he'd be gone too long.

He spent some time dropping into stores and moving along the walk, and he noticed that the general reaction was more of curiosity than anything. He understood why. The people knew him as a piano player and nothing else, and they just couldn't quite reconcile the star with the man.

By the time he got to Big Bessie's Place, Jefford Lane
had left, but some trail hands were there whooping it up,
along with Harry Lane, who was trying to drink his way
down to where he could see the bottom of the bottle
through the neck. The trail hands were more interested
in having fun than making trouble, and the only remark
made was from a gangly boy with the first man-hair on
his face.

"Hey," he said. "You step in something, sheriff?" He
pointed to the cast protruding beneath Shannon's cuff.

"A bee kicked me," Shannon said, smiled and went on.

He stepped to the bar beside Harry Lane, and Elfrieda
turned the faro layout over to someone else and joined
them.

"Beer all around," Shannon said to Mulloy.

"Whisky's my drink," Harry Lane said. His eyes looked
like wet marbles, and he clung tightly to the edge of the
bar as though afraid he'd fall if he let go. He seemed
fascinated by Shannon's badge and finally said, "I could
have had that. You know that?"

"We all know that, Harry," Shannon said. He took his
beer, blew off the foam and clanked the stein against
Elfrieda's. "Here's to the big wind to dry all the tears up."

"I'll drink to that," she said.

Harry poked Shannon with his fingers. "Hey, what you
talk like that for all the time?" He waggled his finger
to indicate both of them. "What's between you two, huh?"

"Finish your bottle," Shannon said. "Then go to sleep."

"I've got five dollars left," Harry said. "Did you know
that? My dear sweet old tight-fisted pappy gave me five
dollars and I'm getting drunk."

Lane's voice was quite loud, and several of the trail
hands turned to glance at him tolerantly. One said, "He's
already made it, ain't he, sheriff?"

"Well on the way," Shannon admitted. He felt annoyed,
but nothing more, and he probably wouldn't if he could

get Harry Lane's big mouth shut. "Mulloy, why don't you fix Harry up with a place in the back room? Give him a bottle on the house."

"I can pay for my own," Harry shouted.

"Then pay," Shannon said. He touched Elfrieda on the arm, intending to move away, but Harry grabbed his collar, slammed him against the bar and held him there.

"I'm not through talking yet."

"But I am," Shannon said. He drove his arms upward, knocking himself free of Harry's grip, and he gave the man a stiff-armed shove that sent him reeling back. "Now you cool down, Harry, before somebody has to paddle your butt!"

"Talk to me like a man," Harry said. "I'm no kid."

One of the trail hands laughed. "Then why don't you stop actin' like one, sonny? Can't you see a good thing when the sheriff gives you one?"

It was the wrong thing to say—well-intentioned, of course but still the wrong thing to say to young Lane, who could only think of the way his father treated him, like some feeble-minded incompetent. He grabbed up the near-empty whisky bottle, fractured it against the bar and turned to the trail drivers.

"I'll fight all of you, two at a time."

"Big brag," one Texan said, and he looked like he was half ready to take Lane up on the challenge.

An older, trouble-seasoned hand said, "Sheriff, better put that boy down before he gets hurt. My boys don't start much in the towns we touch, but we're hell for finishing things."

"Harry," Shannon said, "it's too nice a night for trouble. Put the bottle on the bar."

"To hell with you. I'm going to cut that badge clean off that coat and wear it myself." He made a straight-armed lunge with the fragment of bottle, and several of the trail drivers drew in a deep breath; it would have wounded

Shannon seriously had he not flattened against the bar and let it slide past.

Then he swung a short, stiff punch and caught Harry in his whisky-full stomach, and the young man sat down on the sawdust-covered floor and vomited. The trail drivers all laughed, and the cool one said, "I reckon that you did that just right, sheriff."

Harry's seizures quieted, and he looked at Shannon, who was still standing there watching him, not at all angry.

"You hit me," Harry said.

"Behave yourself now," Shannon warned.

"Put me in jail! Lock me up!"

"Do I have to do that, Harry?"

"You don't dare," Harry said. "You know it, too." He reached for the broken bottle which was not far from his hand, and Sannon came down with the steel loop at the bottom of the cast and pinned Harry's wrist to the floor. He managed to sweep the bottle away by leaning most of his weight on the bar and using his other foot. Then he reached down and pulled Harry to his feet.

"You've got a choice—go home or sleep it off in jail." He looked at the resentment and frustration in Harry Lane's face and knew there wasn't much choice at all; he'd just have to sleep it off in a jail cell.

Elfrieda Danning looked worried. She said, "Why don't you just let him go, Bob?" And even as she asked, she knew it was no good. The trail drivers were watching closely to see what brand of justice they could expect in Cedar Springs, and, whatever happened, they'd tell it down the line. Shannon could rise or fall on what he did in the next moment.

He gave Harry Lane a push toward the door, then marched him on down the street toward the jail. The trail drivers turned back to their fun, and the cool one made a bet at Elfrieda Danning's game.

"That plaster leg don't slow him up much, does it?"

"He does all right," Elfrieda said.

The gaunt man scratched his unbarbered head. "Of course he just handled a drunk. A mean sober man's a mite different."

She looked at him steadily. "He can handle that, too."

The Texan grunted, chuckled and made his bet, and no more was said about it.

• 8

SHANNON HAD AN early breakfast, and, the way he figured it, he'd have some time to kill before Jefford Lane rode storming into town.

Harry was awake, and when Shannon brought him his breakfast on a tray, the young man threw it on the floor petulantly and refused to eat. He also refused to leave and seemed proud to be so stubborn, so Shannon left the cell door open and went back to the office to sort wanted dodgers. He knew from experience that a good place for a wanted man to lose himself was in some cow outfit pushing north; he just sort of got hid by the dust and the noise and the sea of undefinable Texas faces. Out of the batch, Shannon picked three who would be the most likely, men who had never been in trouble before but who got into it good when they did. A man like that didn't know what to do with himself, and, having only one trade, he'd more than likely tie up with a moving outfit, hoping to lose himself among the Yankees. The crimes such men committed were all acts of passion, mostly shootings; very rarely were the crimes premeditated, like robbery or rustling.

Jefford Lane came to town, just as Shannon knew he would, and he marched into the office, his manner as ominous as thunder. "Where is he?" Lane demanded.

"The door's open."

Lane went into the small cell block and looked at his son for a moment; then he whipped his hand across Harry's face. "You weak-kneed pup, you can't even hold your liquor like a man!"

He took his son roughly by the collar, hauled him out of the cell and shoved him down the short hall into Shannon's office. "Are you charging my boy with anything?"

"Not a thing," Shannon said. "He just needed a place to sleep it off."

"Get outside and wait for me! God damn it, do as I say!"

"Tell him to go to hell, Harry," Shannon said softly, drawing Jefford Lane's angry glance, but the young man just shook his head and did as he was told.

After he went out, Jefford said, "What the hell was the idea of saying that?"

"It's all right to put a fatherly hand on his head now and then, Jefford, but don't push him into the ground."

"When I raise a boy," Lane said, "he either turns out a man or I'll find out the reason why. By God, you have your gall, arresting my boy."

"I didn't arrest him," Shannon said. "I put him in a cell so he could sleep; the door was open all night." He spread his hands and smiled disarmingly. "Besides, you didn't give me any instructions on what to do."

"Agggh," Lane said and stomped out. Shannon could hear him talking gruffly to Harry; then they left town.

Shannon felt pretty good about passing the first hurdle, but he knew he had another one, the really important one. He put on his hat and hobbled down the street to the hotel. The clerk was talking to Ralph Palmer, who ran a small once-a-week newspaper, and, as soon as Shannon stepped into the lobby, Palmer buttonholed him. "Ah, Shannon, I'd like a word with you."

"Try good-by," Shannon suggested.

Palmer shrugged off the insult. He said, "Shannon, there

seems to be some conflict between the law and order factions in this community."

"Why, what makes you think that?" Shannon asked. "Just because we had a little argument is no reason—"

"A little argument?" Palmer looked at the clerk, then at Shannon. "Why, the man's still in bed from his injuries."

"Well, I was just going to call on him and see how he's getting along." He smiled, moved past them and thumped his way up the stairs. Cordell kept a room near the end of the hall; he liked it quiet so he could sleep. Shannon didn't bother to knock; he just opened the door and stepped in.

Cordell was in bed, and one glance was all Shannon needed to tell him why the marshal wasn't on his feet. The broken nose had swollen his face so both eyes were tightly closed, and it would be a week before he could see.

"You're a mess," Shannon said, and toed the door closed. "How do you feel, Manning? Mad enough to kill me?"

"That's what you're after, isn't it? You want me to come at you in a blind rage. I'm not going to do that, Bob. Fact is, I'm not going to lift a finger against you."

This was not what Shannon had expected, and he frowned. "Are you going to let this pass?"

"Of course. You merely lost your temper and jumped me. Men will understand how that could have happened. And they'll think it's big of me to forgive and forget. So you can see who's going to look small."

"You're a smart man, Manning. I guess I made a mistake, thinking you'd ever react like any other man." He paused for a moment to think. "But you're not going to just stand there and let me hack away at you, Manning. You've got to fight me, because I'm going to fight you."

"I'll fight you," Cordell said. "But my way. In such a way that you can't fight back. Bob, you can't beat me.

I'll never come to you on your terms, with a gun in my hand. Can't you understand that you're dealing with someone different than you, smarter than you? This isn't the Texas Rangers, where you corner your man and shoot it out with him. You're going to learn a new way, but then it'll be too late." He chuckled softly. "Bob, you don't understand me, and I don't understand you, either. Why are you doing this? Why are you bothering, butting in?"

"It's a good question," Shannon said frankly. "Twenty years ago, when I was a kid, we lived in a place that was a nest for every robber and bushwhacker in west Texas. And nobody did anything about it either. Then one day my father had had all he could take. He left the home place, rode into town, threw the sheriff out of office and put on the badge himself. By sundown he'd posted notice on the toughs, and before the week was out he'd had to shoot three to prove he meant what he said. Two months later they were gone, and he came home and took up where he left off. It was just something that had to be done, Manning; the need is reason enough for some men."

"A very saintly attitude," Cordell said.

"No, it's not that," Shannon said. "Manning, I've raised my hell on the shady edge of the law, but I've worn a badge, too, and I believe in it. That's why I'm wearing one now—and, when the need is gone and you're gone, I'll take it off." He turned to the door and opened it. "Get well, Manning. You'll come after me."

"Don't count on it."

"I am counting on it," Shannon said sincerely. "Manning, I'll make you come after me, on my terms."

He went out and down the stairs, not really believing what he had just said because there was something inexorable in Manning Cordell; he was a fanatic, a grim man wedded to a grim purpose.

Because Manning Cordell was a vain man, he would not

appear on the street while marks of the fight remained on his face. He remained in his hotel room for over three weeks, leaving the town to Bob Shannon.

And Shannon had his hands full. The cattlemen were arriving in constantly increasing numbers, and no sooner had one outfit moved on when another, bigger one arrived to take its place. The main street was a bright, noisy, busy place all night long, and Shannon walked it, watched it, controlled it, using roughness when he had to and gentleness when it would get the job done. Like most men building a reputation, he was unaware of it or, rather, of its extent. Yet he knew that he had the respect of the trail hands, perhaps even their admiration, for though still hampered by the cast on his leg, he asked no consideration because of it. He rousted troublemaking drunks, broke up fights and got into a few of his own. Once he thought he was going to have to draw his gun, but the other man decided it would be better just to leave town; it wasn't much of a place to die in.

Doc Windham soaked the cast on Shannon's leg with vinegar and gingerly cut it away, then bandaged the leg and told him to either stay off it or use a cane. Shannon couldn't stay off it, so he bought a cane and limped through his rounds, sitting down often but not neglecting his duties much.

A good many people in Cedar Springs thought that Jefford Lane had made a good choice in sheriffs, but another faction, who read Palmer's paper and believed everything they read, accused Shannon of being too tolerant, too much "in" with the cowboys. These people were generally humorless do-gooders who wanted quiet all the time, prayer meeting four nights a week and Bible-reading all day Sunday, and the cowboys irritated them mightily.

Manning Cordell's first act was to rent a small place on the main street and have a painted sign hung: *United States Marshal's Office*. The trail hands were a little surprised; they had come to accept Shannon as the only law in town, and it made them nervous to have Cordell around, watching them, saying nothing. He would walk the streets at night, almost aimlessly, or stand in the saloon, chewing his cigar like an eager undertaker waiting for someone to die.

Shannon didn't like it either, but he couldn't do anything. He usually returned to his office just before daylight, and early one morning he found Cordell waiting for him there. Shannon took off his hat and coat and hung them up; then he looked at Cordell.

"Don't you have an office of your own?"

"This is official business," Cordell said. "I want to go over your reward dodgers. There may be some there that come under Federal law."

"I'll let you know if there are any," Shannon said firmly. "Manning, get out of this town. Find some other place to build a nest." He placed his hands on the desk and looked steadily at Cordell. "Get one thing straight, Manning. You'll never make another arrest in Cedar Springs without a Federal warrant. I'm going to see to that."

"Can I quote you in my report?"

"Do as you damned please."

Cordell smiled and stepped to the door. "Thank you, and I'll have a copy of my report on your desk by tomorrow evening."

"Why bother?"

"You'll find it interesting," Cordell said, and walked on toward the hotel.

Shannon sat down and wondered what Cordell's point might be. He sorted through the dodgers and came up with one he'd buried at the bottom of the pile. Brett Carnes, age twenty-three and wanted for murder; the wanted poster was backed by a Federal warrant held in St. Louis. Shannon wondered if Cordell knew about this, but decided that he didn't, for the poster had been in the unopened batch. But

Brett Carnes was in town; Shannon had seen him twice, and he knew which outfit he was riding with.

He had thought of arresting Carnes but had held off because he hadn't wanted to surrender his prisoner to Cordell—and he knew that he would have to sooner or later. Shannon felt certain Cordell would take him and kill him in some way, and he tried to work out a solution.

He supposed he should get to bed, but Cordell's visit bothered him now, so he went to the stable, rented a buggy and drove three miles out of town to the Running T outfit. The foreman was a skinny, ageless man who never smiled and talked only when forced to.

Shannon got out of the rig and walked over to the dying breakfast fire. He accepted a cup of coffee and a plate of beans and fatback, and the foreman waited for the talk to begin.

"You've got a man named Brett Carnes working for you," Shannon said.

"Likely I have," the foreman admitted. "So?"

"So I'd like to talk to him. Officially."

"Suppose he don't want to talk to you?"

"This isn't an arrest," Shannon said.

The foreman thought it over, then sent a man to fetch Carnes. Shannon ate his beans and had another cup of coffee; then Carnes came into the camp. He came up to the fire, but stood in the clear, in case he had to use the pistol he carried.

"In my office I've got a Federal wanted poster on you," Shannon said flatly. "And there's a marshal in town who'd like to arrest you. If he does, you'll never get to trial."

Carnes looked at his foreman, then said, "What's that mean?"

"He'll kill you. He has others."

The foreman chewed his tobacco a moment, then said, "We know you, but we don't know him. What's on your mind?"

"Cordell has access to my files; he'll find that dodger, and he'll find out you're here because merchants in town will remember seeing you. Carnes, I could arrest you, but I don't have a charge. Why don't you light out tonight?"

"Beats me, just what kind of a sheriff you are," the foreman said.

"I'm trying to do what I think is right," Shannon said, "Carnes, I'm not a jury, so I can't decide your guilt or innocence. You may be guilty as hell for all I know, but I'd rather see you light out than fall into Cordell's hands and be shot in the back."

"It was a quarrel," Carnes said. "I thought he had a gun."

"Don't tell it to me," Shannon said. "Just find some other part of the country to light in; this one is worn out for you."

"He's talkin' sense," the foreman said. "I'll pay you off after supper and put you on late guard. That way you'll have eight hours start before anyone misses you." He looked squarely at Shannon. "I believe you because I heard talk about Cordell killin' two young fellows that broke jail."

"There was another up north," Shannon said. "And two more before that." His glance touched Brett Carnes. "I hope you're worth all this trouble."

"I'm not," Carnes said, "but thanks anyway."

He went back to work, and Shannon had another cup of coffee with the foreman.

"We had a lawman down Texas way who had a killin' streak in him," the foreman said. "Someone shot him from an alley one night, and I can't rightly say that much lookin' was done to find out who did it. Could be this marshal will end up the same way."

"I'm working on it," Shannon admitted.

The foreman grinned. "Bet you are at that."

W<small>HAT ANGERED</small> M<small>ANNING</small> C<small>ORDELL</small> the most was his inability to instill in Bob Shannon a proper fear; to Cordell, it was completely illogical for Shannon to keep on defying him when the man knew that Cordell could not be bluffed or bullied.

He wrote his report as soon as he returned to his hotel room because he was angry and because he wanted to write down all the bitter accusations. In the report he accused Shannon of running a loose office, without order or regulated ordinances. Shannon's handling of local affairs was, as Cordell put it, grossly inefficient, and it constantly interfered with the smooth functioning of the Federal office. He recommended then that steps be taken to have Shannon removed before serious damage to the county legal structure took place.

Placing the report in an envelope, he mailed it at the express office and took the copy to the jail for Shannon to get sick over. Finding Shannon gone, he waited awhile, then put the report on the desk. But, before he left, he opened the drawer where the wanted posters were filed and went through them carefully. When he saw Brett Carnes' dodger, he paused and wrinkled his brows. In his own mind he was positive that Carnes had been in town.

This was a beautiful moment for Cordell; it meant that he had a man to arrest and that he had caught Shannon in one of those fatally foolish mistakes the careless always make. He did not doubt that Shannon knew the man was in the locality but had withheld the information, covered it up for reasons of his own.

Cordell folded the dodger, put it in his pocket and left

the office. He knew now that his next report would contain more than unsubstantiated complaint. He now had a case against Shannon, and he would use it wisely.

It took him two hours to ask the questions, show the dodger around town and make up his mind that Carnes was nearby. Learning which outfit Carnes was with, he saddled his horse and rode from town. There was no hesitation in him because he knew what he would do. It pleased him to think that when Bob Shannon woke up Carnes would be in Federal custody and Shannon in trouble.

Cordell boldly rode into the cowcamp and dismounted; the foreman came to meet him, and Cordell came directly to the point. "I'm Manning Cordell, the United States Marshal. I want Brett Carnes."

"That a fact?" the foreman said. A crowd of riders were gathering in a loose circle about them, but Cordell didn't seem bothered by it.

"Is this a resistance to arrest?" he asked.

"If you mean are we going to give up Carnes to you, it sure as hell is," the foreman said.

"What's your name?" Cordell demanded.

"Texas Jack Vermillion."

"The gunfighter? I've heard of you."

"Then it'll pay you to listen," Vermillion said. He stroked his roan mustache and hitched the twin pistols up on his hips a little. "Carnes is here, but you're not takin' him in. I've got thirty men in this camp who'll eat you alive if you bat an eye the wrong way. If you want Carnes arrested, go get the sheriff; we'll turn him over to him to avoid trouble. That way, we know he won't get shot in the back."

The color draining from Cordell's face was the only clue to his profound rage. Finally he said, "All right, I'll get Shannon. The law's got to be served, Vermillion. One way or another."

"We'll take Shannon's way, if it's all the same to you."

"Very well, I'll be back in an hour."

"You don't have to come back," Vermillion said. "Send Shannon, and a bunch of the men will ride in with him to see that you don't do any shootin' from behind a rock."

Cordell pointed his finger at Texas Jack Vermillion. "One of these days the law'll get you, too."

"Sure, but it'll be a better man than you enforcin' it. Now get out of here."

Once away from the camp, Cordell stopped and sat his horse until he collected himself; the violence of his anger made his hands tremble. Then he rode on, thinking of how he would have to handle the situation. He knew how but hesitated, thinking that his solution might detract somewhat from his own importance. He studied all the possibilities, then decided to go ahead with his plan.

This was his frame of mind when he entered town and dismounted. He knew the merchants in this town, the men solidly behind law and order, the man who were his friends and who believed in him. He went to these men and told them about finding Carnes and about their new sheriff, Shannon, who had also known a fugitive walked the streets but had done nothing about it.

He wanted good men for this posse, men he could trust, men who could be deputized and would carry out their duties like trusted law enforcement officers. And they agreed to go with him because he inflated their sense of self-importance and convinced them they were striking a blow against inefficient local law.

Fourteen men gathered quietly at the stable within the hour and, with Cordell leading them, rode toward the Running T camp. Cordell felt sure that Vermillion expected Shannon and not a posse, and was convinced that a daylight raid was so daring a thing that Vermillion would not be at all prepared for it.

They dismounted a distance from the camp, and moved about in a large circle, keeping well hidden. Cordell, from where he crouched, could see everyone in the camp clearly, and he saw Vermillion talking earnestly to Brett Carnes. At least a dozen men were there, all armed, but they did not act as though they expected trouble.

Cordell's shot was to be the signal, and he sighted along the barrel of his rifle, drawing his bead on Carnes' chest. The buttplate rapped him as he fired, and he saw Carnes fall. Then Vermillion made a sprawling dive for cover, and everyone seemed to be firing.

The cowboys ran like scattered chickens, and three of them fell while the others sought cover. Cordell left his position and charged the camp, running down the slight slope to the draw, firing as he ran, followed by his deputies. It was Texas Jack Vermillion who put an end to it; he stopped shooting and ordered the others to stand with their hands raised.

Four men from town disarmed the Texans while Cordell toed Carnes over on his back to observe the accuracy of his shooting. The man was dead, as were three of the other cowboys. Ed Means, who had worked as a clerk in the store, was gasping out the remainder of his life on the slope, where he had fallen.

Cordell walked over to Vermillion, who stood there, his expression like stone. "Well, Marshal, you got him, didn't you?"

"Didn't you think I would?" His expression turned hard, and he seemed to be restraining himself from striking Vermillion. "When I see a man who has to be taken, I take him. I came here and wanted to take him by peaceful means, but you wouldn't have it. If there's blame, lay it where it belongs—on yourself and Shannon." He turned to the men who had come with him. "Get the horses; we'll take these men back with us. I'll press no charges against the others because they acted in haste and on poor advice. Two of you go up the slope and get Ed Means. He's a hero; I want you to remember that."

The cowboys stood around while Cordell and his men got

ready to leave. They kept looking at Vermillion, as though waiting for an order that would start the fight all over again. He said, "Not now. Our time's comin'."

Cordell glanced at him. "Just to keep the record straight —I knew Carnes was here because Shannon gave me the reward dodger. And I went to Shannon with your offer, Vermillion. He said he wanted to sleep and for me to handle it any way I had to. It was too late for me to come into the camp again; you were all set against me by Shannon. So we have a shooting. I'm sorry."

He turned and got on his horse, and they rode out, taking the five dead men with them. Vermillion watched them leave, then he said, "Tonight, when it gets dark, we're going to town."

"To get Cordell?" one man asked.

"Naw, to get Shannon."

Manning Cordell was a master showman. As soon as he and his posse reached town, they tied up in front of his office. The four Texans were left tied to their horses, but Ed Means was brought inside. Cordell got an American flag and draped the body with it.

Then he sent for Palmer, the newspaper man, and everyone had a chance to tell his story while Cordell wrote a report of the affair. Cordell let everyone have his say, and the truth got a little stretched in the process, until it was accepted that the Texans had fired the first shot and Cordell, with splendid courage, had broken their spirit by a reckless charge down the hill. Ed Means, who hadn't done much shooting because he had been scared, was dead and couldn't deny that he alone had killed the other three Texans; no one else wanted to accept the responsibility for it.

Cordell finished his four-page report; he had two men sign each page, then put it in his desk drawer. Ed Means was carried away with tenderness because everyone felt sorry that they hadn't known all along that he was a hero, and Palmer remained to clear up a few details with Cordell.

"When did you first learn that Carnes was in the cow-camp, Marshal?"

"I found a wanted poster, quite by accident, in Shannon's desk."

"Do you mean that he knew Carnes was here and did nothing?"

Cordell held up his hands. "I didn't say that, Mr. Palmer. In spite of our differences of opinion, please remember that Shannon is a fellow law enforcement officer and deserves some consideration."

"That's damned charitable, Marshal, but my readers are entitled to the truth."

Cordell smiled. "Mr. Palmer, you're a fearless crusader. Well, it does seem odd that Shannon did nothing, but it was his affair, and I stayed clear of it. Perhaps he meant to act. I don't know. Still, he failed to inform me of Carnes' presence, and it was a Federal warrant." He shrugged. "I can only relate these facts in my report, which I had witnessed. It isn't my privilege to draw conclusions." He smiled and tapped Palmer on the arm. "I leave that to newspaper editors; they are trained to analyze and editorialize."

"Thank you very much," Palmer said. "Be sure to read my special edition."

"I wouldn't miss it," Cordell said. After Palmer went out he closed and bolted the door, then took the four-page report out of the drawer. The signatures were at the bottom of each page, below a three-inch blank space Cordell had purposely left there. Now he filled the blank space in, accusing Shannon of trying to make a deal with the Texans. When he was finished, there wouldn't be anyone to say that the signing of this report had been forced. None of the men had read it, and it was something that would hold up at a hearing and throw Shannon clean out of the county.

Cordell felt like eating a good meal now. Afterward, he would ride up to Lone Pine, a town to the north, and look around for a few days. Palmer's paper, the report and the angry Texans would be enough for Shannon to face. Cordell wouldn't gain anything by staying around.

Bob Shannon woke just at dusk, which was a little early for him, and he lay in bed a moment or two trying to figure out what had brought him awake. Then he saw the smudge-gray shape of men in the room and reached for his pistol.

Texas Jack Vermillion said, "Touch it and I'll blow you right out of your skin."

"What is this?" Shannon asked. He threw back the covers and sat up. He was wearing only his underwear, and, when he reached for his pants, one of the cowboys pulled the chair out of reach.

"Take his arms," Vermillion said softly, "and don't let him hit the floor. I don't want a lot of noise."

Shannon tried to strike the Texas man nearest him, but he was soon smothered by strong arms and held helpless. Vermillion stepped up and said, "I'm not going to kill you, Shannon. I don't want to hang for this, but it's something for Carnes and the others."

He hit Shannon a solid blow in the mouth and drew blood, and, since Shannon was held by the men on each side of him, only his head was lashed back by the blow.

"We trusted you," Vermillion said. "You lyin' sonofa-bitch."

He was really beginning to show temper now, and he hit Shannon in the stomach, driving the wind out of him, and then snapped him erect with an uppercut.

Vermillion struck Shannon three more times, then said, "Throw some water on him. I want him to remember this."

One of the cowboys emptied a pitcher on Shannon's head, and he shook it, trying to focus his eyes. He looked at Texas Jack, then said, "Why?"

"I wouldn't waste time telling you," Vermillion said, and went to work.

He knew how to hurt a man, and he hurt Shannon without knocking him out. When Shannon sagged, the wash water was poured on him, and Vermillion kept hitting him. Shannon could take just so much; then he lost consciousness and the two cowboys had to hold him up.

One said, "There ain't no more water, boss."

"Put him on the bed," Vermillion said, his breath ragged. He wiped his bloody knuckles on his pants leg and walked over to look at Shannon. "And I trusted him. God damn it, I should have known better."

"He ain't goin' to die, is he?" one of the men asked.

Vermillion shook his head. "Naw, but he'll remember this. Come on, let's get out of here. We'll be five days gone before he feels like comin' after us."

He stepped to the door and, before he opened it, took another long look at Bob Shannon. "It purely is a shame," he said, "that a man don't have more time. I'd like to stand up to him with a six-gun and do it right." Then he sighed. "Well, a man can't have everything."

They went out, and the last man closed the door quietly.

• 10

AT TEN O'CLOCK, when Bob Shannon failed to make his appointed rounds, Elfrieda Danning turned the deal over to a house man and went to the bar to speak to Mulloy.

"Have you seen Shannon tonight?"

"Nope. Maybe the talk's scared him away."

She gave him a withering glance. "If you think that, you'd better find another job." She got a shawl out of the back storeroom, and left Big Bessie's and walked over to the hotel. Without saying anything to the clerk, she went up the stairs and down the hall and knocked on Shannon's door.

"Bob? Bob, are you in there?"

Her hand was on the knob, and it gave a little, which was odd; she opened the door and then fumbled for the lamp. After she got it lit, she turned and saw him near the washstand, face down on the floor, a trail of dried blood marking his journey from the bed. Her first thought was that he was dead; then she rolled him over and saw that he was alive but badly beaten. His face hadn't been marked too much, but his torn underclothes showed her the welts and discolored bruises on his chest and stomach.

She went out and halfway down the stairs and called the chore boy over. "Get Doc Windham and tell him to come here. Shannon's room."

"What's wrong?"

"Never mind. Just go get him, and hurry."

He scurried away, and she went back to Shannon. There wasn't a drop of water in the room, but the rug was soaked. She went out, found an open room, took the water pitcher off the dresser and carried it into Shannon's room. He was stirring and trying to sit up, and she helped him. Her petticoat was nearer than the washcloth, so she ripped off a piece and washed his face.

Shannon, breathing in short, painful gasps, looked up at her. Then he took her hand and held it. "Frieda, you're an angel."

"And you're a fright. Who did this?"

"Running T. Don't ask me why." He touched his stomach and grimaced. "God damn, it feels like my ribs are all cracked."

"The doc's on his way; I sent for him," she said. "And I don't have to ask why this happened. Bob, Cordell killed four men out there this afternoon."

He acted as though he hadn't heard her, but he had. Then he nodded. "It all fits now. Did Manning go alone?"

"No, he took a posse with him. Ed Means was killed."

"Ed? Hell, what was he doing along with them? Come on, help me up off the floor."

"You stay there until Windham says you can move," she said. "The story is all over town about the fight. Cordell's a hero and Ed Means is a hero, and everyone is proud because our local boys licked the Texans."

"Haven't they stopped to figure that the law only wanted one man? What were the others, a Manning Cordell bonus?"

"Nobody stops to figure at a time like this," she said.

Doc Windham arrived and came in. He said, "I like you, Shannon; you're turning into my best customer." He pushed Elfrieda aside and examined Shannon, prodding and pushing and making Shannon groan. "Well, I don't think any ribs are broken, which is a miracle. Although the way things are going for you, a lot of people are going to be sorry that it wasn't worse." He squinted at Shannon. "Some think that if you'd helped Manning like you should have, Ed Means would be alive right now. It's a loss to the town to lose a young man like Ed."

"Oh, for Christ's sake!" Shannon snapped. "He'd been hired and fired by every merchant along the street. He was too stupid to ever be any good and just smart enough to keep from being worthless."

"That's strong talk about the dead," Windham said, closing his bag. "Nothing I can do for you. Stay in bed a few days." He turned to the door and stopped there. "Manning is going to put salt on your tail, boy. And he may make you like it."

"I won't like it," Shannon assured him.

Windham left, and, with Elfrieda's help, Shannon sat on the edge of the bed. "Will you please get my pants?" She handed them to him and he slipped into them, being

careful not to stir up too much pain. "I'm beginning to
understand what Manning meant when he said he was
too smart to come after me the way I wanted him to,
with a gun in his hand. As a kid I've tied a can or two to
a dog's tail, but I never knew what it felt like before."

"You've got to fight him," she said. "Bob, he hasn't
licked you yet."

He looked at her for a moment, then said, "You really
are on my side, aren't you?"

"All the way."

"Why?"

She shrugged. "I don't know. Maybe it's because you
can make me forget all those foolish things I want. Or
perhaps because you're on the bottom and trying to get
up, and I just feel sorry for people in that fix." She stood
up and adjusted her shawl. "I've got to get back to Big
Bessie's Place. Do like Doc says and stay here."

"Uh-uh." He got up, but it took effort, and he started to
finish dressing. "Go on back. I may come in later."

"The Texans aren't in a friendly mood."

"No? Well I'm not in a friendly mood, either."

She left, and he slipped into his coat and put on his gun-
belt; then he went slowly down the hall and took the back
stairs to the alley. He didn't think he'd ever take a decent
breath again, the way his ribs and chest hurt, but this
wasn't the time to baby himself. Not with Manning Cordell holding the pattest hand a man could get.

He lit the lamp in his office and sat down. He found the
report on his desk, and after reading it he threw it away;
it failed to surprise him or arouse anger in him. Manning was going to chew him down from the top, which was
as good as cutting off a man's legs.

Shannon supposed that he ought to walk up and down
the main street just to show the Texas men that he wasn't
afraid of them and to let the townspeople know that he
didn't care what they thought. He'd about made up his

mind to do it when a horseman dismounted outside. Then Jefford Lane stomped in.

Shannon wanted to ask him if he had ever walked without stomping, but Lane didn't give him much of a chance.

"I'm not here about this trouble you're in, Shannon. I've got troubles of my own. Thirty head of stock has turned up missing." He tapped his finger on the desk. "And I want something done now."

"Tonight?"

"In the morning," Lane snapped. "Be at my place at dawn. Harry will be back then; he'll go with you."

"Where is Harry?"

"Oh, out on a tear," Lane said. "He's still sore about what happened a while back. You know how Harry is." He got up, having said what he wanted to say. "Charlotte's at the hotel. I'd go see her, if I was you. Been two weeks since you've said hello. She's hell to live with when she's on the peck about something." He frowned, as though touched by an afterthought. "Oh, yeah. Get this business settled between Cordell and yourself. It looks bad for me when you're on outs with everyone."

"Well, we couldn't have that, could we?"

"You're damned right we can't," Lane said and went out to his horse.

After he rode down the street, Shannon locked the office and walked to the hotel; it seemed to be a very long way. Charlotte would be in the dining room, he knew, and he went there and found her at their old table. He sat down gingerly and hoped she wouldn't say anything about the new welts on his face. She took his hands and said, "Bob, I want you to know that I don't believe a word of it."

"That makes two of us; I don't believe it, either." The waiter kept hanging around, so Shannon ordered coffee and pie for both of them. "The bull of the woods came in to see me. He says he's been rustled."

"Thirty head. The foreman found them missing this afternoon."

"That doesn't mean they were taken then," Shannon pointed out.

"Well, in the last four or five days then, because these steers were part of a bunch that had been cut out and held for shipment." Then she smiled at him. "I don't want to talk about rustled steers."

"Pick a subject," he suggested.

"Love."

"It has possibilities. But it takes two."

"Don't we have two?"

"And a determined father," Shannon said.

The waiter came with the coffee and pie and said, "If you want anything else, order it now. The kitchen is going to close."

"We'll both live until morning," Shannon said, and paid him.

The waiter laughed. "Don't be so sure."

It was just a little thing, something smart that slipped from a mouth that had remained buttoned and had choked back a thousand replies to discourteous customers. But it set Shannon off, and he came out of the chair quicker than he had ever thought he could. He grabbed a bit of the man's shirt and drew back his fist to hit him, but was held back by Charlotte's cry.

"He's just a servant, Bob!"

He released the man, who backed away. Then Shannon sat down and shook his head sadly. "I took this job to get Manning Cordell, and now it ends up getting me. Thanks, Charlie."

"Why don't you come home with me tonight?" she asked. "I've got the buggy, and you can tie your horse behind." She looked at him and smiled invitingly. "Dad won't be home until late." Her hand came again across the table and touched his. "We can talk about love."

"A noble subject," he said. "I'll get my horse and meet you at the stable in ten minutes."

He went out and started down the street, but, before he took ten steps, the crowd of Texans milling up and down had singled him out, and the call passed back and forth. Riders formed a loose ring around him, and two of them even rode onto the boardwalk to block his way.

Shannon stopped and looked at them; then a slender, slight man stepped out of Big Bessie's, paused for a moment and crossed the street toward him.

The crowd seemed to cluster around him as he came, and Shannon suddenly understood that here was a man made special by some particular talent—a man fawned on, catered to, hired when the need was great. When this man stopped ten feet from the street edge, everyone fell silent, and even the riders kept their horses from fretting and moving around.

"You're Shannon," the man said.

"No, I'm President Grant; I just shaved off my whiskers. Who the hell are you?"

"Jim Spade. I'm wanted by the law, so arrest me." He wore a pair of walnut-handled pistols supported by crossed cartridge belts, and Shannon knew that he was an expert with them.

"What are you wanted for, shooting off your mouth?"

He was saying the wrong things as far as Spade and the Texans were concerned; they wanted him to be properly afraid of this man, but Shannon wasn't showing any fear. Spade took off his hat and scratched his head, then put the hat back on.

"Do you know who I am?"

"A damned fool looking for trouble," Shannon said. "Yeah, I know you. When I was in the Rangers you were trying to be a badman down around Dallas. You shot two faro dealers, a sixty-year-old town marshal and two boys not yet twenty. The last I heard of you, you were pimping in a red-light place in El Paso. I suppose they got tired of having you around and kicked you out."

A murmur went through the Texas ranks at this talk, and Jim Spade's eyes grew hard and his mouth pulled into a thin line. "You've bought yourself trouble, Shannon."

"Yeah, sure. I've been buying it all my life, and I'll tell you something you won't believe—you won't be any faster on the draw than the last badman I had buried." He let his glance sweep the Texas men. "I'm going to tell you something, so listen. I've coddled you when you got drunk and treated you decent, so now you sick this gunfighter on me. All right, you want it, because you must have chipped in to pay his fee. Well, you've bought yourself a dead man, with some funeral expenses." His eyes flicked back to Jim Spade, and he said one word. It was enough. *"Go!"*

Spade must have been thinking of his reputation, because he did something Wild Bill Hickok would never have done—he went for both guns at the same time. The left one came out in a hurry and was triggered off into the dirt at Shannon's feet, while the right-hand gun pulled a little to the right, the bullet breaking the arm of a Texan standing four feet to Shannon's left.

When the hammer fell on Shannon's .44, Jim Spade was standing in the right place. The bullet took him dead center, shoulder high, and he staggered back, both guns falling from his hands. He followed them down in a spiraling tumble, dead before either gun hit the ground.

In the stunned silence, only the cursing of the Texan with the broken arm could be heard up and down the street. The mounted men crowded a little closer to look at Jim Spade, who didn't look very good.

One of them said, "He was supposed to be the best, too."

"Mister," Shannon said. "No man's the best. And I won't thank any of you stupid bastards for making me kill a man tonight." He turned and pushed through the

mob, taking care not to let them crowd him too close.
When he was clear, he reholstered his .44 and walked
on, cane thumping, head down. For a moment there he had
hated all of them, because killing a man always added to
the weight already in his mind—and he didn't want the
weight to get any heavier.

Charlotte Lane was waiting in the buggy; she had tied
his horse on behind.

"What was that shooting?" she asked as he got in.

"Somebody tried to kill the sheriff."

"Why, that's dread—" Then she caught herself and
gasped. "Bob!"

He picked up the reins and clucked to the team. "Come
on, let's go. *Yaaaa!*"

• 11

Bob SHANNON WAS HAVING breakfast with Charlotte Lane
when Jefford came back from town; he stomped into the
kitchen and scowled heavily. He hung up his coat and hat
and spoke without turning his head. "When did you get
here?"

"Last night," Shannon said mildly, and drew Lane's unbe-
lieving stare.

"You spent the night in this house? With my daughter?"
He glanced at her, aggravated, aghast; he wasn't sure what
to do about it, what to accuse them of, what to believe.
Obviously he did not trust Charlotte or credit her with any
laudable morals.

Shannon said, "Now I wouldn't accuse anyone of anything
or say too much, Mr. Lane. Sit down—there's some coffee
left." He waited until Jefford Lane obeyed, then shoved the
pot in his direction. "You were about to jump to a conclusion and make a big mistake. I slept on the sofa last

night, but we talked until three o'clock. That's all of our business you need to know." He turned to another subject like a blackjack dealer flipping a card. "My grub's all sacked and my blankets rolled. So if you'll point out the direction the tracks lead, I'll be out of here and doing my job in fifteen minutes."

"I'll have one of the hands show you where the tracks peter out, in the rough country." He drank some of his coffee. "Wish that damned Harry would get back. He could go along with you. Keep him out of trouble."

"That's not part of my job," Shannon said. "But I could use a man I could trust." He shrugged. "Well, it doesn't matter. Your cattle are either on a train East by now or in a smokehouse." He pushed back his empty plate and stood up. "Thanks for the breakfast, Charlotte."

"Ain't you going to say anything about last night?" Lane asked.

"What do you want me to say? A man threatened a peace officer."

Lane shook his head. "They weren't after the badge, and you know it. Shannon, I'd like to say something about that affair."

"Some other time," Shannon said, and went out the back door. His sack of grub was on the porch, and he went to the barn to saddle a horse. He lashed his bedroll in place, along with a heavy coat; there was frost in the air and a hint of snow in the high country. He borrowed a rifle and some ammunition from Lane's gun locker, and was adjusting the boot when Jefford Lane came to the barn.

"When I get something on my mind, I've just got to get it off," Lane said. "Shannon, I want my cattle back and the men who took 'em put in jail. By that I mean I don't want Manning Cordell to have anything to do with it."

"What makes you think I'd let him?"

"You didn't do very good in stoppin' him with Vermillion's outfit," Lane said. He wiped a hand across his rugged face. "Damn it, I don't know where I stand with you. Sometimes I think you like me, and other times, like now, I think you don't. You do right by me, Shannon, or I'll take that badge away from you."

"Now that would be mean," Shannon said, and stepped into the saddle.

He rode out immediately, still favoring his leg and his aching back and stomach. All that day he worked toward higher ground, and for company he had a taciturn rider he'd picked up on the range who was supposed to show Shannon where the tracks petered out. When they began to work their way up a solid rock trail, the rider pointed, grunted and rode on back toward the ranch house.

That night Shannon was deep in the badlands, and he made a fire and watched the sky for the snow he knew was coming. Then he rolled in for the night, using a rock overhang to give him some shelter. He wasn't looking for sign of a herd driven this way; there wouldn't be any, with the trail days old and the country rocky. He intended to move in a northerly direction; there were only two towns near enough to do rustlers any good, both of them serviced by the railroad.

In the morning he found six inches of snow on the ground, and he had to root around a little to find enough dead brush to build his coffee fire. Sitting out there alone, he thought about himself and wondered about himself. The sky, gray and low, pressed down on him, and around him lay desolation; it was the kind of atmosphere that drove a man to look inward to himself. If he were lucky, Shannon decided, he might live to be forty; few lawmen lived beyond that, even with luck. And he wouldn't have much to show for his troubles, either, for the pay was poor, the chances long and the blessings nonexistent. Some woman might be fool enough to marry him, but he didn't think Charlotte would, not as long as he wore a badge. He'd have to get into some other line of work, something with respectability to it;

what it would be he couldn't imagine. Some men, he decided, were simply not trained to be respectable.

With the coffee in his stomach and the fire kicked out, Shannon mounted up and rode on. He figured two days, taking into account the snow on the ground and more on the way, and on the afternoon of the second day he broke out of the pass and started down the slope to the long valley floor. He arrived in town at dusk, stabled his horse, then went to the saloon for a drink and some of the free lunch. This taken care of, he walked to the edge of town to check with the depot agent about any cattle that had been shipped out during the last ten days. The agent thumbed through his records and found that there had been two shipments, both small, with one carload being consigned to the slaughterhouse in Lone Pine.

Shannon, satisfied by this, bought a ticket on the next train out and had the boy take his horse to the depot for loading in a freight car. He had nearly two hours to kill until train time, so he returned to the saloon, bought a bottle and took it to a solitary table. He knew from experience that rustlers were generally stupid; any man who thought he could make a living stealing small was stupid. He reasoned that, with stolen beef, the best and safest thing to do was butcher and get rid of the hides; thus he figured that Lane's beef was in the Lone Pine slaughterhouse.

Dead beef wasn't going to move any farther, and, since the men who sold them would relax now, figuring that the worst was behind them, Shannon did not feel particularly rushed. He drank enough whisky to begin to feel it, then went to the depot to sit outside in the cold to wait for his train. He heard it finally, a long way out, hooting and puffing along the valley floor; than he saw the yellow glare of the kerosene lamp as it neared town. It clanked and steamed into the station, disgorged passengers and shuffled a bit on the siding to pick up two freight cars and load the mail car; then Shannon got aboard and found a seat.

He put his ticket in his hatband, tipped the brim over his eyes and went to sleep. The jolting of the coach didn't bother him, and the chatter of other passengers didn't disturb him, but, when the train slowed for Lone Pine, Shannon woke up.

On the station platform he walked up and down to keep the cold from biting his feet; then his horse was taken from the freight car, and he mounted to ride toward the center of town, which was one block long and one street wide with a scattering of houses filling in to the south. The saloon was open, and the hotel lobby still sported a few glowing lamps. Shannon tied up in front of the hotel, registered and took his key, then walked across the street to the saloon. He didn't really want anything to drink, but, if a man wanted to know anything, he had to go where information collected.

The place was like a stall, with the bar running the length of the building and all the poker tables going on in the back room, through an archway hung with beads. As Shannon waited for his glass of beer, he could hear talk and laughter and the slap of cards. Then he cocked his head to one side and listened more carefully—he had recognized a voice.

Taking his beer, he sauntered toward the archway and peered in. Harry Lane was at the table, and had obviously been there some time; he had all the signs and the tense face of a steady loser. Shannon watched him for only a moment; then he went back to the bartender, who was alone.

"Some game, huh?" Shannon asked.

"Been going on since early afternoon. The kid's stubborn. He won't lose fast."

"He looks like he's been losing," Shannon said.

"Yeah, nearly two hundred dollars, but only a few dollars at a time. Slick-Eared Thompson's determined, though. It's the first big one he's had in here all week. Suckers are hard come by these days." He winked at Shannon. "You feel lucky?"

"I'm never lucky," Shannon said, finishing his beer.

He recrossed the street to the hotel and found the clerk asleep behind the counter. Without waking him, Shannon pulled the register around and searched until he found Harry Lane's name and room number.

Quietly going up the stairs, Shannon walked along the dim hall until he found Lane's room, tried the door and then went inside to wait. There was no doubt in Shannon's mind now as to who had taken the cattle. Harry never had any money, or at least not enough to lose in a big poker game; this meant only one thing to Shannon, and he was sorry as hell that it did.

Shannon settled himself on the bed to wait, thinking what a damned shame it was that he couldn't lock the old man up for this instead of arresting the boy. Harry had been squeezed too tightly, and it had figured that he'd have to make his break sometime, in some way. Too bad it had to be this, though.

He slept lightly, in snatches, and woke when he heard Harry Lane's step outside the door. The young man came in, closed the door and leaned his back against it; Shannon could hear him breathing in the total darkness. When he tried to get off the bed, the springs protested, and Harry jumped.

"Who's there? I've got a gun!"

Shannon could either freeze or move, and he didn't like staying still. Harry tried to get the door open, but Shannon grabbed him and they rolled on the floor, Harry trying to use his gun and Shannon clinging to his wrist to keep him from using it. They upset a small table and rolled half under the bed; then Shannon banged Harry's head against the floor a few times, got possession of the gun and released Harry to light the lamp.

Lane blinked, stared at Shannon and said, "What the hell are you doing here? What is this, anyway?"

Shannon threw Harry's pistol into one corner of the room, then motioned for Harry to get to his feet. "Sit down. We've got some talking to do."

"What did you jump me for?"

"You're nervous, Harry, and you've lost all your money."

"How do you know that?"

"Because you're a fool, and fools always play until their last cent is gone. How many head did you sell? The whole bunch?" He sat on the bed and looked at Harry Lane. "I've caught my share of rustlers in my time, but you're the dumbest I've ever seen. You drive north, where there's only two places you could sell the beef, then hang around and spend the money. Who was in this with you?"

"I did it alone."

Shannon shook his head. "Harry, one man couldn't drive thirty-odd head across the pass with the first snow of winter breathing down his neck. Now how about it? Are you going to name the others? Or am I going to have to hunt them the hard way?"

Harry thought about it a moment, then shrugged. "What the hell difference does it make, Bob? They were from Vermillion's outfit—they wanted some easy money. They've gone on north to Bent Fork by now. One of them had a girl there."

"I'm going to have to take you back, Harry."

"So? The old man will make you turn me loose."

"He's mad. Don't count on it."

"I can count on one thing," Harry said. "He'll cuss me and take a strap to me and call me a no-good sonofabitch, but he won't let me stay in jail, because I'm a Lane."

"Do you think people will stand for me arresting the other two and letting you go scot-free?"

"It's your problem," Harry said. Then he laughed. "I finally did something without the old man's hand on my

shoulder or having his blessing. He ought to be pleased, because he's always told me I couldn't do anything by myself
—and he's spent his life proving it." He patted his pockets
for tobacco and found none, so Shannon tossed him his
own sack of makings. After Harry had a smoke going, he
said, "I'm not going to give you any trouble going back,
Bob. I want to go back, to see his face when I tell him that
I rustled him." Then his manner grew more serious. "Say, it
would really be something if I did my time in jail, wouldn't
it? By God, he don't think I'm man enough to do it, but I
could show him. I sure could."

"That's the hard way to prove something," Shannon said,
"but I guess it's the only way for you." He sighed and
rubbed his thighs. "You're under arrest, Harry. The charge
is cattle rustling. But I want your two friends, too, so what
do I do with you? Chain you to a tree until I get back?"

"You could trust me to go back by myself," Harry said.
"Bob, it kind of figures that I've got to go back, if I'm to
prove anything to myself."

"Yeah, I guess it does," Shannon said. "But I'm really
gambling on you, Harry. You could cross me and fix me
good."

"No, I only want to fix the old man."

Shannon, with what he was going to do settled in his
mind, got off the bed and stretched to ease his sore muscles.
"I ought to be back in four days. Be here."

"I'll be here," Harry Lane said. "You're damned right I
will."

Shannon went out to the street, more troubled in mind
than he should have been; this bothered him, made him
restless. Catching up his horse, he rode slowly out of town
and spent two hours moving around it in a sweeping circle,
as though giving his back trail and the other avenues a
good looking over. Then, satisfied that he was not being
followed, Shannon cut onto the trail to Bent Fork, having

decided he ought to wear out the rest of the night cutting down the miles.

With his horse picketed in the brush, Manning Cordell hunkered down in the ink shadows of a huge tree and watched the town and the trail leading into it. He waited with an endless patience, and in time he was rewarded; he saw a rider moving cautiously, searchingly, and in the faint night light he recognized Bob Shannon. After Shannon passed from view, Cordell waited half an hour longer; then, chuckling to himself, he mounted up and rode on into town. He got a deep sense of satisfaction out of outsmarting another man; it took brains to trail another without being detected, and, while Shannon was clever, Manning Cordell fancied himself infinitely more so.

Entering the town, Cordell tied his horse and walked up and down the street in order to look things over. He stopped, looked inside the small marshal's office and one-room jail and saw that it was empty. A pause by the saloon window assured him that his man wasn't there, and, since the hotel was the only other place open, Cordell approached it with an air of confidence.

He disturbed the clerk's reading and said, "My brother's got a room here. A young man, twenty or so, rather good-looking."

"Oh, sure. Third door on your left, mister."

"Thank you," Cordell said, and went easily up the stairs, walking on the balls of his feet. He paused just outside the door, speculating on whether he should try the knob or just ram it with his shoulder. He put his hand on the knob and turned it, and the door opened; he swung it wide, and Harry Lane started to get off the bed. But, as Cordell drew his gun, Harry stopped and looked at the marshal.

"I could pull this trigger now," Cordell said, "and never be blamed for it." He sidled into the room, disarmed Harry and thrust the gun into his waistband. "You're under arrest, Harry."

"Hell," Harry said, "I'm already under arrest."

Cordell's eyebrow lifted. "Shannon arrested you? And you're still armed?" He laughed and shook his head. "Don't hand me that."

"We made a deal," Harry Lane said. "I'm going back alone. He went after the other two who were with me."

"Now isn't that sweet," Cordell said. "If I let you give yourself up, it would make Shannon out to be quite a lawman, wouldn't it?"

"I don't see that," Harry said. "You do your job your way and Shannon does his another." He studied Cordell. "What are you going to do, Manning?"

"What do I always do?" Cordell asked softly.

Harry Lane stared at him for a minute, his complexion pale. "You wouldn't kill me, Manning. My old man would skin you alive."

"I'm not afraid of your father," Cordell said. "Or of any man. Look at it my way, Harry. If I bring you in after Shannon arrested you and then turned you loose, it would make a fool of him. But, if you're dead, Harry, who's going to say that Shannon didn't shoot you?"

"There are people who'd never believe that of him!"

"Sure, there always are, but your old man would believe it. He'd set the dogs on Shannon." He motioned with the muzzle of his gun. "Let's go, Harry."

"No!" Harry said. "Manning, you could make a deal! The old man would give you a lot of money!"

"It isn't money I want," Cordell said. "A lot of men can make money. A fool can do it if he's lucky. Come on, Harry, we're wasting time."

"Kill me here!" Lane said, jumping to his feet. "Kill me here where the shot will be heard!"

"All right," Cordell said softly, and, leveling his pistol,

he sighted it right between Harry Lane's eyes and held it there for a full minute.

"God, please don't!" Harry pleaded, and closed his eyes; his nerve had broken. Cordell smiled, having gambled that it would. He forced Lane down the back stairs; they got Harry's horse first, then went around in front for Cordell's. They left town together, attracting no attention at all.

Finally Harry said, "Won't you give me any chance at all, Manning?" Cordell didn't answer him, and, when Harry stopped and turned his horse, he saw Cordell standing motionless in the middle of the trail. The lights of the town were still faintly visible a half mile behind them, and Cordell, pulling the trigger, was certain that no one would hear the shot.

Then he holstered the pistol and dismounted to go about the tedious business of loading and tying Harry Lane face down across the saddle.

• 12

No MATTER WHICH way Shannon looked at it, his horse was going to need a couple of days in a box stall with some good grain in his belly before he'd be ready to ride back. And, while Shannon was hanging around town, it wouldn't be a good idea to keep that sheriff's star pinned to his coat; he took it off and put it in an inside pocket.

Finding the stablehand agreeable, Shannon paid for stall and feed in advance, then went to the hotel to get a room. He slept out the day, woke with a hellish hunger and, out of habit, gravitated to the free lunch counter in the saloon. The night trade was beginning to drift in, and Shannon never gave the other customers a second glance. He was, in his way, practicing manhunting the way he had learned

from the Rangers—doing everything as quietly as possible and with the least amount of fuss. The men he
was looking for were, in a way, complete strangers to
him; he could not describe them, yet he felt certain he
would remember their faces from having seen them in
Texas Jack Vermillion's camp that one time.

Shannon had not shaved or beat much of the dust from
his clothes, because he knew how anonymous a saddle
tramp was; and, since the two men he sought had seen
him, too, any change in his appearance would help him.
He remembered that one time he'd chased a man clean
across Texas, having nothing to go on but a description
from a wanted poster; and, when he had finally made
his arrest, he realized how much walking with a stoop
fooled people.

He drank beer, played solitaire and walked up and down
the street like some itinerant getting the lonesomeness of
the hills out of his system. It was an easy three days, and
he looked forward to Saturday night, which ought
to bring all the riders in from the outlying ranches; Shannon was now sure that the men he was looking for had
either moved on or had found a place in some local
bunk house.

So he'd give it one more whirl, and, if nothing turned
up, he'd shave, put on his badge and ask the local marshal
if he'd seen two riders in town with money to spend. This
wasn't the only time he'd been saddled with a cold trail;
matter of fact, he'd never really been on a hot one, so it
didn't bother him to pick up something two or three
weeks old.

The town sported a lively crowd on Saturday nights, and
the stores stayed open late. Shannon kept moving around,
keeping a particular eye on the saloon. Finally he saw
two men whose faces were familiar in a store, buying
some clothes. Shannon ducked down the street and into

the marshal's office. When he presented his badge, the marshal didn't seem at all surprised.

He said, "When I see a man hanging around for three or four days, I usually look at him twice. I figured that, if you were the law, sooner or later you'd be coming for me. And, if you were wanted, I'd be coming for you."

"An interesting theory," Shannon said. "Will you help me arrest two men? I want to get the drop on them and prevent shooting."

"Do you have a warrant?"

"I've got a man under arrest who'll point his finger."

The marshal smiled. "Sometimes that's better than a warrant." He picked up his gunbelt and stepped to the door. They walked down the street together and reached the store just as the two cowboys were coming out. Shannon's nod was enough to alert the marshal, and, when the two men stepped to the edge of the boardwalk, Shannon made his move. He jerked the pistol from one man's holster and shoved the muzzle of his gun into the rib cage of the other.

"Say, what is this?" one of them asked. Then he got a good look at Shannon. "Well, if it ain't the sheriff!"

"Buck, Larry—what you two boys been up to?" the marshal asked.

"Cattle rustling," Shannon said. "I caught Harry Lane."

The two men looked at each other; then Larry said, "The sonofabitch talked; I knew he couldn't keep his mouth shut."

A small crowd was beginning to gather, and the marshal said, "Let's go to my office."

The two men were herded inside, and Shannon held them there while the marshal went to get their horses; he liked to see trouble moved on out of his town as soon as possible. Shannon studied them a little sadly; they were young and foolish, and they'd have to pay plenty for being that way.

"We're not going back to be hung," Buck said flatly.

"You're going back," Shannon said softly. "I can't say what the jury's verdict will be. But you're going back —bound hand and foot, if it has to be that way."

There was no more talk until the marshal came back. "No sense keepin' them here all night," he said.

Shannon grinned and said, "You don't like trouble, huh?"

"Well, I really don't have enough of it to know. There's nothin' to keep you here, is there, sheriff? That is, you'll bunk as comfortable in the hills as in town, and I won't have to buy these two breakfast."

"I know—it comes out of your pay." Shannon motioned for the two men to step outside and mount up. A small crowd began to gather, but the city marshal moved the people along. Shannon tied both men's hands to the saddle-horn.

The one named Larry said, "If my horse stumbles, how do I kick free?"

"Ride carefully," Shannon said, and swung up. "All right, ride ahead of me." He crowded their horses into motion and trailed them out of town.

He kept them riding for five hours; then they stopped for a cold camp. Shannon seemed calm, sure of himself and not particularly worried about whether he should sleep with one eye opened or not. He did take off his gun-belt, though, and double-buckle it in his saddlebag, giving them no chance to grab it quickly; and, if they did make a break for freedom, he would have time to get himself up and take a shot before they hauled out of sight.

Shannon was Texas-Ranger trained; in the Rangers it was not uncommon for a lone man to escort six dangerous fugitives clean across the state and get there safely, without having to shoot a couple along the way. And he knew how to get his sleep every night without worrying about his prisoners. Of course, he did expect trouble from them. Buck had a big mouth, and he promised Shannon that

he'd better not try and get any sleep because he'd be
jumped if he did. Buck figured that, if they could wear
him down until he was dead on his feet, he wouldn't stand
much of a chance against them.

Shannon let the threat ride the first night, but on the
second he introduced a idea new to them. Their hands
were bound behind them in the usual fashion; then their
horses were brought up, and, with the prisoners on the
ground, flat on their back, their right feet were tied to
the stirrups.

"Now," Shannon said. "I'm going to sleep fine tonight,
and both of you are going to stay awake, talking to
your horses to keep from being dragged."

"This is cold-blooded murder!" Buck wailed.

"Not unless you fall asleep and let the horse spook,"
Shannon said, and rolled into his blankets.

In the morning he helped two bleary-eyed men into the
saddle, and they moved on. A few days later, when they
reached Cedar Springs, Buck and Larry had given up
any idea of escape. In fact, the cots in the jail cells
looked most inviting.

Shannon washed, shaved, changed his clothes and tried
to forget his disappointment in Harry Lane, who had obviously gone back on his word. Now he'd have to hunt
Harry down and bring him back with his hands tied.

Locking the jail, Shannon walked to the center of town.
The lamps were coming on, and he noticed that traffic
was unusually thin on the street. Bits of paper tacked to
the walls of all the buildings caught his eye, and he
walked over and tore one off a wall. He read it once and
didn't believe it, then read it again to make sure.

I, JEFFORD LANE, OFFER ONE THOUSAND DOL-
LARS IN CASH, ALONG WITH THE SERVICES OF
THE BEST LAWYER MONEY CAN BUY, TO THE

MAN WHO WILL SHOOT BOB SHANNON ON SIGHT.

Wrinkling the paper and tossing it in the street, Shannon said, "He's gone crazy," and hurried on to the saloon. Every customer in the place looked at Shannon as he came in. Elfrieda Danning was standing by the bar, reading a paper, but she put it away as soon as she saw him. Then she motioned toward Bessie's room, and he followed her back.

Bessie was sitting in her easy chair, smoking a cigar. She spoke when Shannon closed the door. "Either you're a damned fool to come back or you're as innocent as a baby."

"What the hell did Jefford post me for?" Shannon asked.

"I knew it was a damned lie," Elfrieda said. "Bob, Manning Cordell brought Harry Lane back to town. The usual way—only he says that you killed him and left him alongside the road. Manning claims to have found him, and he says Harry spoke your name before he died."

"Why, that sonofabitch! I left Harry in the hotel room; he promised to come back here and give himself up." He saw the question in their eyes and gave them the answer. "I see how it is. The old man won't believe my story about Harry rustling the cattle. Sure, it figures. Manning has made a real smart move, but I've got the other two rustlers in jail. They'll tell the jury Harry was along."

"Jefford Lane still won't believe it," Bessie said. "Honey, why don't you just skip the country and save yourself some trouble? I know you didn't do it, but, what the hell —you can't prove it. Besides, Manning has played his ace."

"What ace?"

Elfrieda said, "He's wired for another U. S. Marshal to come and arrest you, Bob. He sent it about three days ago, from some town north of here." She sat down and massaged her fingers together. "Bob, why would he do that?"

"I'll have to ask Manning," he said, and turned to the door.

"I wouldn't go to him," Bessie said. "I'd get out."

"Sure, it would be the smart thing to do, but I've never liked being chased up a tree."

As he passed through the saloon, the customers stared at him, their manner hostile. Crossing over to the hotel, he went up the stairs and knocked on Manning Cordell's door. When Cordell opened it, Shannon saw that he had interrupted the marshal's shave.

"Well, I always said you had nerve," Cordell said. "Come on in." He turned to the washstand and finished blading his cheeks clean. "Did you see the posters? I asked Jefford not to do that, but he went ahead anyway." He wiped his face and threw the towel on the bed. "Bob, why couldn't you have taken my advice to begin with? I'm going to have to arrest you."

"Go ahead," Shannon said. "This one will be more than you can handle."

Manning Cordell smiled. "*I* won't arrest you. That might not look too good, in view of the trouble between us. So I've asked a man to come in; he ought to be here late today." He spread his hands in an appealing gesture. "Bob, you're licked. I've done everything in my power to help you. I even had Jefford Lane put under a five-thousand-dollar peace bond to keep him from shooting you, so you can see no one would believe that I've been anything but most just." He picked up his shirt and put it on. "Shannon, I'll give you a break. Turn in your badge and leave the country, and I'll withdraw the charges. That's more than fair." He shrugged. "What the hell, I'm going to have your God-damned badge anyway; the rest I'll throw in as a favor."

"No," Shannon said softly. "You want to do it your

way, but it's not what I want, what I have to have, Manning. Come at me with a gun. Do it like a man."

"You Texas men are all alike, very fundamental." Cordell took his watch from his pocket and glanced at it. "Roughly, I'd say you had less than eight hours."

Shannon studied the marshal for some time; then he flicked his .44 out of the holster and cocked it, holding the muzzle steady on Cordell's belt buckle. "What's to keep me from finishing this right now?"

"All those years as a Ranger," Manning said softly. "You wouldn't shoot a United States Marshal, not with what you have to back it up."

"You're right," Shannon said, opening the door. "But you're going to come for me, Manning, with a gun in your hand."

Cordell smiled and shook his head. "Not a chance, Bob. Good-by."

Shannon slammed out and down the stairs. On the street his rage cooled a little, and he began to think clearly, to work on a way out of the mess he was in. While he was on the street the southbound stage wheeled into town, and a crowd gathered to look over the dismounting passengers. A rancher embraced his wife and two daughters; then a spare man got down, looked in both directions, got his bag from the boot and went into the saloon.

Shannon walked to the stable then, rented a horse and rode out of town a few minutes later, taking the road to Jefford Lane's place. He wondered if he was a fool for even thinking he could talk to Lane, but he knew he had to try. If Lane believed the truth—and there was only slight hope of that—then he might throw some weight Shannon's way and nullify Manning Cordell's damning case.

Or maybe Lane's rage would get the best of him and he'd shoot Shannon himself; that would be a miserable way to die—innocent, put upon, a complete failure in the job he'd set out to do.

Yet he'd take the chance; it was better than running.

Then he thought of Charlotte; surely she couldn't believe Cordell's lies. He felt better, thinking about her, and lifted his horse into a brisker pace, arriving at Lane's shortly before ten o'clock.

There didn't seem to be anyone in the yard when he rode in and dismounted, but, when he stepped onto the porch, he heard a rifle receiver open and close behind him.

A man said, "Go on in, but I'll be right behind you. And keep in mind how good a thousand dollars looks to a man who's never made more than thirty a month in his whole life."

"I'll remember," Shannon said. "You want my gun?"

"No, you can keep it; I've got you covered."

Jefford Lane heard their voices and flung open the door. He stared at Shannon for a full minute; then he hit him, knocking him back across the porch, over the rail and into a bed of sun-dried flowers.

"Get him to his feet," Lane said, his voice a rumble in his throat.

The man with the rifle collared Shannon and kneed him forward. Lane hit him again, driving him to his knees. Charlotte came out, then, pushed her father back against the wall and held him there until reason returned to him. He was breathing through his mouth, like a man who has run both far and fast, and he kept staring at Shannon, killing him over and over again with his eyes.

The cowboy said, "All right, fella, you've been down there long enough. Stand up." He poked Shannon with the rifle muzzle and stood back when Shannon got to his feet.

Charlotte looked at him with tears in her eyes. "Bob, how could you have done it?"

He let the hurt show. "How could I? You think I shot arry?"

"Well, what am I to think?" she asked. "Tell me." e wiped her eyes on her apron. "Why did you come re?"

"To tell you I didn't do it," he said. "And to find some- e who believed me, I guess."

"Harry's dead. He can't clear you, Bob."

"I didn't think he had to," Shannon said. Blood dripped om his nose and ran down his chin. He looked at Jef- rd Lane. "Why don't you give him the thousand and t him shoot?"

"I'm thinking of doing it myself," he said.

At that moment a horseman rode into the yard. Lane rked his attention away from Shannon and spoke to the wboy. "Go see who that is and send him on his way."

"Right," the man said, and trotted away. He met the rseman before he could reach the porch. "This is private, ister. Come back some other time."

"I'm the United States Marshal from Laramie," the man id. "Bill Stagg's the name. I was told in town that heriff Shannon rode this way." He looked at the group anding on the porch, with the parlor light behind them, en rode past the cowboy and stepped from the saddle. He oked at Lane, at Charlotte, then at Bob Shannon. "You're hannon, aren't you? I'm afraid you'll have to come back town with me."

"We handle our own troubles here," Lane snapped.

Bill Stagg looked at him for a moment. "You're Lane? Vell, Mr. Lane, the government takes a different view. Get n your horse, Shannon, and wait for me." He gave hannon a shove. "Go on, man. The ice isn't heavy enough o hold both of us."

Jefford Lane spoke to the cowboy with the rifle. "Murphy, f he puts a foot in the stirrup, shoot him."

"That would be a serious error in judgment," Stagg said.

He popped his elbow against his side, and a double-barrele derringer snapped into his palm, released by a gambler' trick holdout rig. "I'm not very fast on the draw," Stag admitted, "but no farther than we're standing from one an other, Mr. Lane, this will be as lethal as a forty-fiv Colt. Tell your man to withdraw, but to leave the rifle o the porch. I'll give you no more than five seconds."

Sighing, Jefford Lane waved his hand. Murphy came u to the porch, laid the Winchester down, then walked an grily to the bunk house. Shannon stepped into the saddl and waited for Stagg.

The marshal said, "In the morning, I'll have your poster taken down. We don't do things like that, Mr. Lane. Goo night."

"Wait!" Lane said, and started toward the edge of th porch, but Stagg was instantly alert, ready for trouble. An Jefford Lane knew it; his shoulders slumped, and he wheele and went into the house.

Charlotte said nothing, and Shannon didn't think it wa his place to say more. Bill Stagg reined close and nodded and they left the yard together.

• 13

MARSHAL STAGG SEEMED TO BE in no hurry to get back to town; he walked his horse, lolled in the saddle and talked. "Marshal Cordell has sent my office several reports on you, Shannon. Sooner or later I'd have had to come here to in vestigate. The shooting of young Lane has only speeded things up a bit."

"Manning Cordell's a liar," Shannon said.

Bill Stagg looked steadily at him. "I've been a law of ficer for nearly eighteen years, and anything I hate worse

than a criminal is a crooked peace officer. Any man who
hides behind his badge has little consideration coming."

"So why don't you shoot me? Manning Cordell shoots all
his prisoners. You read the record. How many men has he
sent to jail? How many has he put in a grave?"

"A man can have bad luck," Stagg said. "There are some
that I've had to bring in across a saddle."

"But not all of them," Shannon said. "Marshal, have you
hung me in your mind?"

"No," Stagg said. "I only arrest a man and gather
evidence."

"Then keep it in mind that Manning could be lying and
that I'm telling the truth."

"What evidence do you have to support that?" Stagg
wanted to know.

"None," Shannon said flatly. "Not a damned thing."

"Then what do you expect me to do, Shannon?"

"I don't know," he said. "What happens now?"

"I'll have to hold you in jail," Stagg said. "Naturally, I'll
investigate the charges, but it's up to the people of the town
as to what happens. If Jefford Lane wants to prefer charges,
there is no way I can stop him."

"Lane could swing any jury picked," Shannon said.

"That may be true, but I can't help it. For God's sake,
Shannon, what made you shoot the boy?"

"I didn't," Shannon said. "I did not shoot him!"

Stagg sighed as though he had come across men like Shannon before, men who would not change their story in the
face of a mountain of evidence. He said, "All right, Shannon,
you stick to that if it makes you feel better."

Stagg knew how to bring a prisoner into a town and get
him in jail without stirring up a fuss, and, when he locked
the cell door, he said, "Shannon, I'm not against any man.
If there's anything good to be said for you, I'll hear that, as
well as the bad."

"Do you want me to live to stand trial?" Shannon asked.

Stagg frowned. "What do you mean?"

"Keep Cordell away from this cell then."

"Marshal Cordell has stepped out of the case," Stagg said. "I'm completely in charge."

He went out, locking the outside door but leaving the lamp on the office desk burning. Shannon sat down on the bunk and let a dismal sense of defeat sweep over him. If this was the way a man felt when everything was stacked against him, then he felt sorry for all those men on whom he had closed the door and turned the key.

He slept miserably because his face hurt from Jefford Lane's blows and his head ached from thinking so much. When the gray light of dawn woke him, he felt as though he hadn't slept at all.

Stagg brought him his breakfast, left the tray and went away. Noon came, and Shannon had to battle the urge to try and kick the wall down. Then someone hit the bars of his window with a stick, and he stood on the cot to look out. Elfrieda Danning was in the alleyway.

"The new marshal's been with Cordell all morning," she said. "I'll bet Cordell's giving him an earful." She tried to make a joke of it, but there wasn't anything to joke about. "Jefford and his girl came into town. They're at the hotel. He took his posters down."

"Any more dreary news?"

She came up to the wall and reached up to curl her fingers around the bars. "Touch me, Bob. I'm scared. Do you think that Marshal Stagg would take a bribe? I'd give him all the money I have."

"You'd have to start all over, Frieda, and you're not the patient type."

"I guess I've given up that notion," she said. "It would never have worked out, anyway." She withdrew her hands. "I've got to go, but I'll be back."

The cell was a miserable, lonely place after she left, and Shannon tried to get some sleep and forget the mess he was in. The day was cold and raw, and he wished someone would come in and build up a fire.

Right after dark, Bill Stagg came in with the supper tray. He said, "You've got a visitor. I'll leave the cell door open and give you thirty minutes, but I'll be right outside."

He stepped to the outer door and motioned, and Charlotte Lane came inside. She took off her coat and the heavy woolen scarf she had tied around her head and came to the cell door.

"I couldn't stay away," she said softly.

"Did you come here to swear at me?" Shannon asked.

She shook her head. "But if you want to swear at me, I have it coming." She clasped and unclasped her hands, then asked, "Is it all right if I step inside?"

"If you don't mind being in jail," Shannon said. He got up so she could sit on the bunk. "Charlie, I didn't shoot Harry." He supposed it was a foolish thing to say, but he felt that he had to tell her once more.

"I know you didn't," she said. "Believe me, I always knew it, deep down inside. Only I was hurt, and I failed you when you needed me. Can you forgive me for that?"

He sat beside her and put his arms around her only because she needed comforting, and he thought how strange it was—this deadness of emotion, this lack of feeling for her.

"I suppose your father's uptown picking the jury," Shannon said.

"He just can't face the truth about Harry," she said. "I'm sorry for him."

"Can you face it?"

"Yes, I believed it from the beginning, and that hurt, too." She raised her lips and kissed him briefly. "What can I do for you, Bob?"

"Nothing," he said, "except watch Manning when I'm gone. Watch him and believe all I've said about him, and, in time, you may catch him. Or somebody may."

She studied him for a moment, then got up and went to

the front door; she knocked and said, "Marshal, will you step in a moment?"

The key turned, and Stagg stepped in and closed the door. They both walked back to Shannon's cell, and Stagg's manner was puzzled, although careful; he was a man very sensitive to the possibility of a trick.

"When we came into town," Charlotte said, "I thought I could smell snow in the air. It'll be the first this year."

"So?" Stagg said.

"So I thought I'd mention it," she said. "Marshal, you've talked to a lot of people. Have you come up with anything?"

He shrugged. "Well, yes and no. As far as I can tell, the town's about evenly divided." He leaned against the bars and crossed his arms. "Shannon, you've got a lot of people here on your side, but the fact that a man is well-liked can hardly be called evidence. Now, Manning Cordell is heading the other camp, and his opinions are backed up considerably. He's got that report of the trouble at the Texas cattlemen's camp, and it's signed by witnesses, which is strong indication that you didn't do your job right, just as he claims." His glance touched Charlotte Lane. "And your father has swung over to Cordell's camp. If this comes to trial, Shannon, and I see no reason why it shouldn't, you don't have much chance of beating it. Jefford Lane really throws his weight in this town. Of course, it figures, him carrying such a large pay roll."

"You don't think Bob has a chance, do you?" Charlotte asked.

Bill Stagg was an honest man; he shook his head. "Not much."

"He's innocent," she said flatly. "He didn't kill my brother."

"Well, maybe he didn't, but where's the proof?"

"Yes," she said dully. "I see your point. May I go please?"

As Stagg stepped away from the wall to reach out and

open the cell door for her, Charlotte suddenly grabbed his arm by the elbow, pressed the concealed trigger there and popped the derringer out of the trick rig. Before he could stop her, she snatched it up and pointed it at him.

"Now this is real foolish," Bill Stagg said.

"Just sit down," Charlotte Lane warned him. "I can shoot this as well as you can. Sit down and listen, Marshal." She waited until he obeyed; then she stood with her back to the cell wall, the small .41 two-shot still pointed at him. "Manning Cordell killed two young men for stealing horses. He claimed they tried to fight arrest, but Bob says they were unarmed. I know they didn't have a gun when they left town, because I saw the jail break and I saw Bob fight with one of them and disarm him. I ran up the street, yes, but I could still see it. Bob was knocked down, and they wrestled on the ground; then the man ran, and Bob picked up his gun. Marshal, he had every right, every chance, to shoot that man down, but he held his fire. I saw this, and, if he tells me that my brother was alive when they parted company, I believe it."

"Cordell says that Shannon made no effort to stop the man."

"Cordell lies!" Charlotte snapped. "Cordell and Shannon went after them, but Bob's horse stumbled, and he broke his leg. Later, Manning stopped out at our place with two dead men. He claimed they put up a fight. But with what? Neither had a gun."

"Cordell told me all about that," Stagg said. "Miss, you'd better give me that gun."

"Oh, no," Charlotte said. "Manning Cordell is a killer, and somehow we're going to prove it. Bob, you're going to escape. Winter's coming on and traveling is going to be rough, so you go to that line shack in the rimrock country above our place. And stay there."

"I'll come after you," Stagg said.

"No, you'll go with him," Charlotte said. Both men looked

at her, puzzled. She explained. "Manning will take up the trail; he loves to pursue a man, to hunt him down. And he'll find you in the cabin, Bob, and then the marshal will see for himself whether or not Manning likes to take a prisoner back dead or alive."

"It won't work," Shannon said. "Manning is a good tracker. Two sets of tracks will warn him off."

"Yes," she said, "you're right. I hadn't thought of that."

"Give me that derringer," Shannon said, taking it from her hand. "I am going to escape, Marshal. And I'm not going to take any food along, or a gun. I'll hole up in the shack, like Charlie suggests. If you want to learn the truth about Cordell, then go with her. She'll take you home and show you a back way to get into that country. I'll be there when you get there—no gun or anything; you can search me if you like, or take me back right then. But, if you really want to find out what kind of a man wears that badge, stay under cover and wait for Manning to show up."

"How could I explain my absence from town?" Stagg asked.

"I'll say that you're going home with me," Charlotte said. "I've invited you for dinner."

Bill Stagg thought about this. "I'm taking all the risks; if this goes sour, I might as well turn in my badge."

"No," she said. "Bob's taking all the risks because Manning will try to kill him."

"You seem sure of that," Stagg said.

"I'm gambling Bob's life on it," Charlotte said. "Marshal, if I'm wrong and Manning doesn't show up, do you see what Bob stands to lose?"

"He'll be out of jail and on the run," Stagg said. "I'll have to catch him all over again."

"Stagg, if Manning doesn't try to kill me, if he doesn't show up to take me, I'll turn myself in." Shannon looked at the derringer he held. "You think I like this, pointing a gun at a marshal? Hell, my old Ranger captain would dress me down good if he ever heard about it."

"When I got Cordell's first report on you, I wired Texas," Stagg said. "You had a damned good record there, Shannon. That was one of the reasons I came here, to find out what could change a man so much." He wiped a hand across his face. "It looks like I'm going to have to trust you—and you to trust me." His glance touched Charlotte Lane. "If Manning Cordell even suspected, the whole thing would fall on its face."

"I know," she said.

"Better tell your father that you're going home and that you've invited me out for a meal. Make sure somebody hears you; I want Marshal Cordell to get the bait."

"Shall I go now?"

Stagg nodded, and she went out, closing the door behind her.

"When you come to the shack," Shannon said, "bring something with more pop to it than this." He lifted the derringer. "Manning isn't going to let you get close enough to use it. He'd kill you, and me, and tell everyone we must have fought it out before he got there."

"You'd accuse this man of anything, wouldn't you?"

"Only of the truth," Shannon said. "Sorry, Stagg, but you've got to have a lump to show for this." He belted the man flush on the jaw, without pulling his punch. Stagg slammed into the cell bars and slithered to the floor, thoroughly stunned. Then Shannon tossed the derringer on the floor, grabbed his coat and hat on the way out and mounted Stagg's horse.

He took the back way out of town, knowing that the marshal would spread the alarm. He wondered what excuse Stagg would think up for not taking the trail that very night. Manning wouldn't wait; he'd move while the tracks were still warm.

For three hours Shannon worked his way deeper into the

rough country. The night air was cold, and around midnight a sprinkle of snowflakes began to fall. He wished that making the break unarmed hadn't been part of the bargain, because, if Stagg made a mistake and missed the line shack, Shannon would be a dead man before he was found.

Shannon didn't know what time it was when he reached the place nestled in the rocks, but the snow was three inches thick and still coming down. He put his horse up in the small lean-to barn and went inside the cabin. Figuring it was safe to light the kerosene lantern for an hour or so, at least, he rummaged around to see what he could find to eat. He found half a pound of bacon and built a good fire in the tin stove. While the bacon crackled in the skillet, he made some hot cakes from flour and water, and filled his stomach to a satisfying level.

Then he put out the lantern and sat in the warm darkness. The heat in the room melted the snow on the roof, and it leaked through in steady droplets, pattering on the bare wood floor. He supposed it had been a little foolish to build the fire, because Manning would notice the snow gone from the roof and draw the correct conclusion that someone was inside. It would be the same as though Shannon had hung out a sign.

To hell with it, Shannon thought, and he curled up in the bunk to get a little sleep. He didn't know when Stagg would get there, if he ever got there, but he had to go on believing that Stagg would show up with a rifle. Of course, Stagg could prove the whole thing by just staying in town, and, if Manning Cordell brought him in dead, Stagg could arrest him. And, if Shannon was brought back alive, he'd be right back where he started.

This was a sobering thought, and he considered it. Manning was as smart as an old coon, and, if he figured just this once to curb his killing instincts, Shannon would be up the wild creek with no paddle. Bringing a man in alive at a time when a senior marshal was on the scene, would make a big impression and zoom Manning's stock sky high.

Well, it just couldn't happen, Shannon decided. A man couldn't live so wrong as to have it happen that way, losing because he was right. He had to go on believing that Manning would fall for it, come at him the way he'd always wanted him to come, with a gun in his hand.

But it sure was a miserable feeling not to have something in hand to shoot back with.

Shannon didn't sleep well at all.

● 14

SHANNON EXPECTED the snow to let up a little the next day, but it continued to fall, a fine powder that was steadily turning the high country a solid white. There was one window in the shack, a small piece of dirty glass that offered only a partial view of the back trail, and Shannon spent considerable time there, looking out.

He hadn't built up the fire again because he wanted a layer of snow to form on the roof; then he got tired of shivering in the cold and chucked pieces of wood into the stove door. Let Cordell see the bare roof; the whole idea was to draw him in, wasn't it? Shannon found no pleasure in telling himself this, because, unless Bill Stagg arrived, Cordell would murder him.

Where was the marshal from Laramie? Shannon fumed and stewed; the man should have arrived hours ago. Could he have been wrong in judging Stagg? Was the man going to sit on his rump in town and let Cordell carry this thing through? It was a grisly possibility.

Late in the day, Shannon thought he saw the dark shape of a far-off rider working his way into the higher country, but he caught only a glimpse—enough to frighten him but

not enough to tell whether it was Stagg or Cordell. He
thought then that perhaps Cordell had found Stagg wan-
dering around, guessed his purpose and done away with
him. Manning Cordell might make his story stick, if he
blamed the death of Stagg on Shannon. And it didn't take
any great mind to figure out how easy that would be.
Shannon had broke jail, hadn't he? He must have scooped
a gun on his way out, and, when the brave Stagg trailed
him and got too close, Shannon shot him from ambush,
then went on—to be shot down by Cordell, who would not
give up until he got his man.

And all it would prove was that Shannon was a killer
who got what he deserved, that Stagg was careless and
that Marshal Manning Cordell knew his business.

After digesting that bit of logic, even the fire failed to
warm Bob Shannon.

In late afternoon he heard a sound outside and went to
the window to see who it was. Manning Cordell was dismounting and tying his horse a short distance from the
shack, and all the time he never took his gaze from the
building. When he approached he did so with his pistol
drawn, and he stopped just outside the door.

"All right, Bob, I know you're in there. Do I have
to kick the door down?"

Shannon felt as though his chest were being squeezed in
a vise; then he got hold of himself and decided that, if
he was going to die, he'd do it to Cordell's face like a man
not like some hiding animal.

Slipping the wooden bolt, he flung the door open. Cordell came in, his manner wary. Seeing that the shack
had only one room and that there was no place for a man
to hide, he toed the door shut and leaned against it.

"Well, it looks like you finally got your wish," Cordell
said.

"What was that?"

"You got me to come after you with a gun in my hand,"

Cordell said. "But what makes it nice for me is that you don't have any." He smiled. "Of course you and I know that, but no one else does." With his free hand he unbuttoned his heavy Mackinaw and exposed another pistol thrust into his waistband. "You took this from the office when you made your break. Which made a dangerous man of you."

"So dangerous you had to shoot me," Shannon said. He didn't find it easy, standing there looking down the muzzle of Cordell's gun, but, once he put his mind to it, it wasn't so bad. The knowledge that he was going to die had been digested, bitter as it was, so what could frighten a man who was already dead? "Manning, one of these days, someone is going to stop you. You've killed too many men who never had a chance."

"Yes," he said, "it bothers me some, but it's a means to an end. Next year I'm going to run for a higher office and put all this behind me." He smiled. "You're taking this better than Harry Lane did; he was really scared."

"Do you think I'm not?" Shannon shook his head. "Manning, you said you were going to put this behind you, but you won't. All your life, as long as you live, you're going to be seeking revenge for your father and brother, and killing a man is like only one drink to a drunk—the satisfaction wears off quickly and he's got to do it again."

"You may be right," Cordell said bleakly. "Well, every man does what he has to do, doesn't he?"

"Then do it and get it over with," Shannon said. "I've dangled long enough. Besides, it's going to be a cold ride back to town."

Manning laughed and raised the gun slightly; then he lurched forward drunkenly as Bill Stagg's shoulder hit the outside of the door. Manning Cordell triggered off a shot, but Shannon was launching himself into a tumbling dive, trying to get past Cordell and out the door. Stagg had burst into the room, and he was raising his rifle when

Cordell caught his balance, whirled and drove him to his knees with one shot.

He flung a belated shot at Shannon, who was outside and running for the cover of the rocks. Then, without a backward glance at Stagg, Cordell left the cabin. Knowing Shannon was unarmed, he had no fear of remaining in the open.

"Better come out! I can find you!"

Shannon crouched in the cover of rocks and listened to Cordell's voice bounce in echoes off the hills. He risked a peek and saw the marshal standing there, keening the air like a dog, and he knew what he had to do but wondered if he could. Easing from one cover to the next, Shannon began to edge around, hoping to get onto the rock overhang that all but butted up against the back of the shack.

Footprints were easy to follow in the snow, and after a minute Manning Cordell began tracking Shannon. This was the time to move, even if it meant exposing himself, and Shannon ducked from cover to cover, hoping he could stay ahead of Cordell.

Stagg was still in the shack, badly hurt; Shannon had seen him drop, and he kept thinking of Stagg's rifle and how much he needed it. There was no chance of leaving the rocks and making a run for the door; Manning Cordell would pot him like a yokel at target practice.

Yet he had to get that rifle, and, to get it, he'd have to get into the shack. The rock overhang near the rear edge of the shack was flat and completely in the open, and, as Shannon made it and crouched there for a moment, Cordell raised up eighty yards away and took a shot at him. The bullet whined off a nearby rock, and Shannon made up his mind in an instant. In one plunge he went off the overhang and onto the roof of the shack. He felt the flimsy structure give; then he went free, rolled and landed in the snow by the door. Cordell shot again, hastily, and missed him; then it was too late for another shot, because Shannon was inside, scooping up Stagg's rifle.

The Laramie marshal was half lying, half sitting, a hand clutching his bloody side. He said, "I deputize—you in—the name—"

"Save it," Shannon said and went belly flat by the door. He levered a shell into the receiver, shouldered the weapon and searched over the sights for Manning Cordell. He caught a glimpse of him and triggered off, feeling the belt in his shoulder as the .40-82 recoiled. The shot was enough for Cordell; he ducked his head and kept it down, and Stagg, half dragging himself across the rough floor, tossed Shannon a full box of cartridges.

"There's seven—in the—gun," he said. "Get him!"

"Now don't think for a minute I won't," Shannon said.

He whipped to his feet and ran for the rocks, and Cordell fired twice more, coming close but not close enough. Then Shannon was crouched against cover, and the fight took on a different complexion.

"Manning!" he yelled. "Throw down the gun; it's over!"

"Not yet," Cordell said. "Bob, you really have it your way now, don't you?"

"Yeah, my way," Shannon said. He knew he just couldn't stay where he was; he had to take the fight to Cordell, and take it all the way.

He started climbing into the rocks, and Cordell started to back off. He didn't want to risk getting into pistol range; his only thought was to get away from that heavy-caliber rifle.

One thing about Cordell—he didn't stop thinking. He led Shannon away from the shack, then abruptly switched around and cut his own back trail. The first thing Shannon knew, Cordell was running for his horse and making a clean break from the clearing. Hurrying back, Shannon was too late to take even one shot at the fleeing man, so he gathered up Stagg's horse, picketed a few hundred yards away, and went into the shack to help the wounded marshal.

An examination revealed the bullet had taken a glancing path; it had ripped up Stagg's side but had not damaged him internally. Still, the wound was ugly, and the man had a rough ride ahead of him. After bandaging him tightly, Shannon helped him outside and onto his horse.

Stagg said, "Go after him."

"I will," Shannon promised. "We'll get you to Lane's place and in bed first."

"I can make it."

"Sure, and I'll go along to see that you do. Manning left me on my own once, and it was real rough." He took up the reins, mounted up and led Stagg back toward the valley floor.

At times all the marshal could do was lie on the horse's neck and hang on to the saddlehorn, and Shannon moved as slowly as possible, although he was in one hell of a hurry. It was well after dark when they reached Lane's ranch, and the old man came out to the porch when he heard them dismount.

"Give me a hand here," Shannon said. "The marshal's been shot."

Jefford Lane didn't understand this, and he didn't want to, but for Bill Stagg's sake he helped lift him down and carry him inside. Charlotte came from her room, saw them and opened a bedroom door; she threw back the covers as they eased Stagg down.

The marshal took Bob Shannon's arm and said, "Don'—waste any—more time—here. You get—Manning."

"Manning?" Lane growled. "What the hell is this?"

"Manning's a killer, you old jackass," Shannon said. "I told you all along."

"I'll send a man in for the doc," Jefford Lane said, and went out.

Shannon looked after him, then said, "He still doesn't believe it."

"He has a hard time changing his mind," Charlotte said. "Bob, will you give me five minutes to get ready?"

"Ready?"

"I'm going in with you," she said. "Manning is in town, isn't he? That's where he'd go, wouldn't he?"

"I think he would," Shannon said. "Manning has to have public opinion on his side; it's a weapon he'll use to stop me or slow me down."

"That's why I've got to go along," she said. "I'm a Lane, and, if I speak for my father, people will listen. Give me five minutes." She dashed out just as Jefford Lane was coming back; he turned to watch her run down the hall.

"Where's she going?"

"To town with me," Shannon said. He looked at the old man and wished that he could make the truth a little easier to take. But it wasn't the kind of surgery that would work with Lane. "Jefford, it's your fault Harry took those cattle."

"My fault?" Lane bellowed.

"By holding him down so tight, by never letting him be his own man. Blame yourself, Jefford. It's your fault." He turned his head and looked at Bill Stagg, who was taking it all in. "Marshal, you tell him."

"He knows," Stagg said. "That's what makes—it so hard." He paused to breathe heavily. "Do you have any whisky?"

Charlotte came back, shrugging into her heavy coat. She had changed from a dress to a pair of man's pants and a wool shirt. "I'm ready," she said. Then she looked at her father. "You could come, too, and tell them that you were wrong, that Harry was wrong and that Bob did the right thing. No—I guess you couldn't do that."

She turned and left the bedroom, and Shannon followed

her. One of the hands fetched a horse for her, and they swung up together and rode out.

There was hardly a powder of snow on the valley floor, but the wind was cold, announcing that a full winter was lurking just around the corner. Once away from the Lane place, they slowed to a walk, for Shannon's horse was tired. It didn't seem that she was ever going to say anything, so he asked, "How did Jefford take it when he found out you broke me out of jail?"

"He flew into a rage," she said. "And the only reason he didn't beat me was because I'm a girl. When you brought Marshal Stagg in, it was the first time we'd spoken since you left Cedar Springs. I don't hate him, Bob. I just wish he could understand." She fell silent for a moment. "I kind of dread telling him that I'm going to marry you. I don't know that he can take that. He wants so much for everyone, and it isn't possible, Bob."

He edged close to her and put his arm around her briefly then he urged his horse to a faster pace because he had very important work to do.

When they reached town they both stopped. Charlotte said, "I'll go in first." She studied the darkened buildings only the saloon and hotel were open for business. "Give me five minutes at the hotel; I'll try to talk Burrage into closing it. That'll leave only the saloon—and every dark alley." She suddenly took his hand and clung to it. "I'm a coward; let Stagg handle it when he gets well. You've treed him, Bob."

"Sure, but I want to knock him out of the tree now," Shannon said.

She knew how useless it was to argue with him, so she eased on down the street, drawing up in front of the hotel. Then from across the street a blossom of muzzle flame brightened a gap between the buildings, and Charlotte's horse reared and fell. Shannon whipped up the rifle and put a shot somewhere near where Cordell was hiding.

he hurriedly dismounted he realized why Cordell had fired.
Charlotte, in man's clothing, had been mistaken for Shannon and Cordell was overly eager to get his killing done.

The size of the muzzle flash and the booming crack
as the weapon had discharged told Shannon that Cordell
had picked up a rifle to even out the disparity in arms.
He sprinted for the other side of the street, and Cordell
triggered off another shot, the bullet snapping the dirt near
Shannon's feet. Then he was on the sidewalk, and, with one
swing of the rifle butt, shattered a door pane, enabling
him to reach inside and open up the door. Only he didn't
go in. He moved to the edge of the sidewalk and caught
Manning Cordell flat-footed. The man had thought that
Shannon was going through the store to come around behind him in the alley—and this was what Shannon wanted
him to think.

"It's all over, Manning!" he shouted, and Cordell pawed
to a halt.

They seemed to shoulder their rifles together, only Shannon triggered the .40-82 off before the metal buttplate
touched him. Cordell, jerked completely off his feet, whipped
into the hitching rail like an old limp blanket and fell over
to lie face down in the street.

Lights seemed to come on all at once, and doors opened
and people poured out; a few held lanterns high, and they
formed a circle around Manning Cordell, who was still
alive.

"Get me out—of the gutter," he begged. "Please—get
me out."

"Lift him to the walk," Shannon said.

They obeyed him, but one man said, "You'll hang for
shooting a marshal, Shannon."

Charlotte, pushing her way through, heard what the
man had said. "He didn't kill my brother. Cordell did.
Marshall Stagg's at our house. Cordell shot him."

This was a Lane, the provider for half the town, talking,

and it set the crowd to murmuring. Cordell was being lowered to the walk, and he was in his final agonies. Shannon stepped up to him, then knelt. "I tried to tell you, Manning. Why didn't you listen to me?"

"Couldn't," he said. Blood was bright on his lips, and more was spreading underneath him from the gaping hole the .40-82 had torn all the way through him. He looked at Shannon for a moment, and there was no blame at all in his eyes; and in that last moment he was the old Manning Cordell who had clerked in the courthouse—a nice, gentle man, devoted to his work.

Shannon decided it was a nice way to die.

A horse thundered down the street; then Jefford Lane used his bull voice and his heavy hands to batter his way through to the walk. He looked at Cordell and rage came to his dark face; then he kicked Cordell, hard, in the ribs.

Charlotte slapped his face. The blow was sudden but not hard, and Jefford Lane turned to her with only shocked surprise.

"You hit me," he said. "Why?"

"Because I want to give you something for Harry, for all the thoughtlessness, the hurt, the overbearing bullying he took from you. And it was for me, too, because I'm never going to set foot in your house again. Do you understand that?"

Shannon stopped her by putting his hands on her shoulders and turning her in the direction of the hotel. He got room for her, took her upstairs and made her go to bed.

Then he went down to the lobby and found Jefford Lane there. The man's face was bleak; Shannon had never seen him this way before, so completely beaten.

"Please," Lane said. "Sit down, as a favor, Shannon."

"I didn't know you ever asked people favors, Jefford."

"I am now," he said. "Shannon, I don't want to lose her."

"Seems that you already have."

"But she's all I've got!"

"So was Harry," Shannon said.

"I know," Lane said. "I destroyed him, didn't I? God, how can a man make a mistake like that?"

"It takes some doing, but you managed."

Lane looked at him. "You hate my guts, don't you?"

"No, I feel sorry for you." He got up and buttoned his coat. "I'm going to marry Charlotte, Jefford. I'm going to go back on our deal."

"Who the hell cares about the deal," he said. "I'll talk to Stagg, though, about getting you appointed U. S. Marshal."

"You do, and I'll cram the badge down your throat." He went over and peered closely at Jefford Lane. "Can't you understand that we don't want you to interfere? Who needs you now? Who ever really needed you? Harry sure didn't. Charlotte doesn't. You think about it."

He went outside and stood on the porch. Cordell was being carried down the street, and the crowd was breaking up, going home. Big Bessie came out of the saloon, and Elfrieda Danning was with her; she saw Shannon standing there and came over.

"Why didn't I think of breaking you out?" she asked. "Are you going to marry her, Bob?"

"She's a real woman," Shannon said. "I love her, Frieda." He reached out and touched her. "Get out of Bessie's place, Frieda."

"What will I do?"

He shook his head. "Something, I don't know what. Go some place else and open a laundry or get married and raise kids."

"Another two years and I'd have enough money to get the farm I first wanted," she said. "Two years goes by pretty fast."

Then she turned, walked back to the saloon and went inside.

Shannon waited a moment longer; then he re-entered

the hotel and went up the stairs. The door to Charlotte's
room was unlocked, and he stepped inside. She had the
lamp turned down and she raised herself halfway into a sitting position when he closed the door.

"Your dad's downstairs," he said. "He needs you, Charlie."

"Does he? Or does he just think he does?"

"You could see him, judge for yourself."

She brushed a strand of hair from her face. "I don't
know, Bob. After all that's happened—"

"It's easy to start a thing that can be hard to stop," he
said. "Are you going to do to him what he's done to you
and Harry, close him out?"

She braced her elbows on her knees and put her face in
her hands. Then she said, "Ask him if he'll come up."

A smile came to Shannon's face, and he came over to the
bed and put his arms around her and kissed her, and she
clung to him for a moment before he pushed her gently
away.

"That is the right thing to do, isn't it?" she asked. "It's
what you want me to do, to forget all of it and start over."

"Sure. That's the way we live our lives; we mess it up,
then forget it and start all over." He gave her a final hug,
then got up and went to the door. "I'll see you in the morning. We've got plenty of time now."

Then he went out and took the stairs two at a time, feeling fine now, better than he could ever remember having
felt.